SERQET

A BUG, A BROTHER, AND
A GREAT BIG BOMB

by N. A. Fulton

No Better Friend Entertainment LLC

Copyright © 2020 Nancy Ann Fulton

All rights reserved

The characters and events portrayed in this book are fictitious. Any similarity to real persons, living or dead, is coincidental and not intended by the author.

No part of this book may be reproduced, or stored in a retrieval system, or transmitted in any form or by any means, electronic, mechanical, photocopying, recording, or otherwise, without express written permission of the publisher.

Printed in the United States of America

CONTENTS

Title Page
Copyright
Serqet
Chapter 1 1
Chapter 2 13
Chapter 3 30
Chapter 4 49
Chapter 5 73
Chapter 6 112
Chapter 7 136
Books By This Author 139

SERQET

Dedicated to F. M. Fulton, an engineer who changed the world who had a brother he loved very much. I miss you, Dad.

--NANCY FULTON

CHAPTER 1

An RV, pulsing with loud rock music, races down a country road toward a dark desert town.

Eddie Maxwell, a late-twenties guy with unkempt black hair, big eye glasses, and a foil hat, checks his mirrors as he swerves the antiquated RV through empty streets that belong in the 1950s.

At one corner he banks particularly hard. Brakes squeal and the RV tires ram into a curb right next to a mailbox. The RV tips slightly and just barely manages to right itself

Eddie scrambles out of the driver's seat. He rolls down the passenger side window and squeezes a thick envelope coated in $1 postage stamps into a mailbox. Something inside the bulky package rattles. As the mailbox door bangs shut, a wave of static hits his radio. Eddie leaps back into the driver's seat and lurches the RV back into motion, working to put as much distance as possible between himself and the mailbox.

The RV careens wildly around several hard corners, then hits eighty as it heads up a highway ramp. Eddie, now driving ninety on the wrong side of the empty freeway, scans his mirrors as wave after wave of static hits the radio.

Then a flash of something black and bright blue in the passenger side mirror catches his eye. Several bikes with blue neon wheels, moving way too fast, are riding up behind the RV. The static from the radio has become continuous.

Eddie looks ahead. There's another ramp coming up, a gas station, a truck stop, both lit up like this is still the twenty-first century. They are just a half mile ahead and twenty feet down from where he is now. The gas pedal is already jammed to the floor, but now Eddie stands on it.

Maybe he is not going to die tonight after all.

Something vicious slides up outside the window on his side of the van. It's a black clad rider on a sleek black machine that runs as quietly as an electric scooter. Eddie looks down and the rider looks up. A stylized steel eagle on the rider's helmet glints. Eddie gives the rider the finger.

A second black rider races past the passenger side

window. He slaps a hand sized flat black disk to the hood of the RV and drops back. Eddie's engine seizes up as if it is suddenly made of concrete.

Eddie jerks his steering wheel hard to the right, doing his best to hit the flying rider closest to him with the whole side of his RV. He jams on the brakes as the vehicle begins skidding sideways down the freeway,

The tortured RV tumbles, rolling over and over again, eventually coming to rest across two lanes of traffic on it's left side. Inside the van, the windshield is shattered and Eddie is lying on his back looking up at the passenger side window, his head pillowed on broken glass. Blood is pooling under him, creating a red corona around his head. His tin hat now looks like a halo.

A black rider gets off his space-age bike and walks to the overturned vehicle. He bends down and pulls off his steel eagle helmet. He peers through the broken window. Fifty-something, with snow white hair, white eyebrows, and piercing blue eyes, this guy looks every inch the efficient military operative he is.

* * *

Richard Maxwell, a handsome thirty-something businessman who looks much like his little brother, is dressed in a bright yellow heavy-weather coat. In his hand he holds a tablet computer displaying black and white security footage. Sleet strikes the window beside him, shards of ice glittering like glass in the high powered security lights that illuminate this cliffside construction office in the newly independent nation of Arunachal Pradesh which has managed to tear itself away from both China and India in recent years.

A stern faced, slightly rotund, middle-aged project manager watches the video over Richard's shoulder.

In the security cam footage it is daytime and a gentle snow falls on a dam under construction. Several workers in bulky insulated coveralls are precariously placed to help guide a huge waspish turbine into a hole on the dam's smooth face. The ugly multi-ton unit swings from a long thick cable, and as it moves closer to the open pit in the wall, workers see a bomb has been attached to it. Shoe-box sized clumps of C4 are wired to a radio receiver.

As the workers signal frantically to the crane operator to back the turbine away, the bomb explodes. The security cam video shakes. Intermittent images show the turbine falling, the crane falling, and several workers falling too.

Richard hands the tablet back to the project manager and looks out the window at a gaping hole in the dam through which water spills. The turbine and the remains of the crane are lying half in and half out of the water at the base of the dam many hundreds of feet down.

Richard shakes his head and turns to look at the Project Manager and the five team leaders in the room behind him. They look a little like bees in their yellow parkas and radio augmented helmets.

"Well, we all know they can tear the dam down faster than we can build it," Richard says carefully.

"This project is absolutely essential. It must go forward," the project manager says firmly.

Richard sighs. "Haziq, you do not have a technical problem here. You have a political problem and a security problem. There's nothing I or my resources can do to help you."

"If you and your company pull out you are making a political decision. One that will impact millions of people. You will be starting an insurrection."

Richard looks at the assembled men. They all look bone weary and cold. He looks out at the hole in the dam. The truth is self-evident. "I'd say a revolution is already begun."

"Please Richard, a few weeks is all we need to get back on track," says Umar. He is the engineer who invested more than a year creating designs and specifications that met Richard's production requirements.

"That is completely inaccurate Umar, because the attacks will continue," Richard replies.

The Project Manager turns and pulls a set of large drawings toward him. It's open to a page of numbers. Richard looks at it and for a moment, inside his head, the numbers swim, change color, flash and crawl in a way that's more than second nature. It's first nature, written into his DNA, and he can't help seeing what he sees.

Two figures stand out. He points to the entries on the page.

"The attack cost you six point three million. You are losing more than four hundred thousand every day that construction is stalled."

The project manager points to another number. "It is only one point four million to repair the dam and rebuild the housing."

Richard looks at the man, hearing an echo from childhood that makes his skin crawl with old revulsion.

"And how much does it cost to rebuild all the men

who were killed?" he asks.

"We will lose as many men as it takes to move this project forward," replies the project manager stoically. This is a man used to getting things done despite incredible adversity, a man who does not admit defeat no matter how much it costs others.

"Not with my help," Richard replies firmly.

"You cannot let a small number of unreasonable people control the fate of a nation!" the project manager, face suddenly red with fury and eyes narrowed by an accusatory rage.

Richard shakes his head, buttons up his coat, and looks around at all the assembled men. He hopes his next words will eventually become not an epitaph but a benediction.

"Didn't you know? It's always the crazy people who make history."

* * *

Paige, a beautiful thirty-something photojournalist, sits in an elegant and sunny kitchen. She's perched in front of a large monitor and she is uploading images onto her computer. Soft music plays while she works. She is looking at her images from a war zone in Africa. Mothers weeping. Children starving. Bodies by the roadside. An oil refinery on fire.

The phone rings and the answering machine picks it up.

“Richard Maxwell. Please leave a message after the tone,” it says as it has several times this afternoon. When people can’t reach Richard by email or cell, they try every method in their database including his home phone.

“I’m calling from Milkwood Community Hospital in Las Trenos New Mexico. I am sorry to say that Eddy Maxwell was admitted this morning at 2:45 AM. He’s in grave condition and it’s critical that you contact us.” The woman on the other end of the phone is clearly used to delivering horrific news calmly. She has mastered a voice that is serious, urgent, and calm all at once.

Paige scrambles to get out of her chair and snatches up the phone.

“Hello? Eddie Maxwell? Are you sure you have the right number? I don't know any Eddie Maxwell.” Paige can’t imagine anything worse than getting this kind of phone call about someone in her family, and already her mind is racing as to how she might help this woman connect to the right Maxwell wherever he might be in the world.

But what the woman says next stops her cold.

"Yes. I guess Richard Copernicus Maxwell is a pretty unique name," she says. Apparently they are looking for Richard, and this terrible call has come to their little family. Her mind is reeling as she wraps her head around what the woman is saying. "I didn't know he had a brother."

Paige checks her pockets, goes to a workstation table, and picks up her cell phone. "Okay, go," she says, then records the number as it is given to her. "Thank you," she says once it is done, "I'll have Richard call."

Paige hangs up and stares at her phone, torn between rage, confusion, and pity. Then she hits a speed dial number. She has the only number on earth that always gets to Richard no matter where he is or what he is doing.

* * *

Richard is being driven across an airport tarmac toward a private plane. It's the middle of the night and the sleet has turned to rain. His cell phone rings and he answers it with a click.

"Yes?" He listens for a long moment, turning his head to look out the window at his waiting plane. As the car pulls to a stop, he opens the door. This miserable frigid rain, this abyss of a tarmac intermittently blasted by long gusts of cold wind, this is an appropriate moment to hear about Eddie, the gaping hole in his life that he has filled with a hundred other things.

He walks into the wind and rain toward his executive assistant who waits at the top of the steep steel stairs with a tablet computer in hand. It's daytime on the other side of the world and doubtless there are fifty calls waiting.

Richard mounts the stairs as he speaks, "I'll be there in fifteen hours Paige. I think I would rather call from home." Whatever has happened to Eddie, it's happened to a stranger who insisted on living his life on the edge. He needs time to steel himself to remember his brother is a stranger and that he chose the course that has led him here.

"Yes. I do have a brother. I am sorry I haven't mentioned him. We don't speak. We haven't for many years. We're less than strangers Paige. I am literally the last person on earth Eddie would turn to for help." Richard mounts the steps, shaking his head as she demands he call now. That is what he won't do. There's nothing harder than burying the living, and that's what he had to do with Eddie. To open that grave requires him to deal with choices he built his life on. That is not a thing he can do in an instant. "I'll explain when I get there."

Richard terminates the call, steps into the airplane, and takes his seat on the private plane. His aide offers him a drink and proposes a meal. Richard waves him off, stares out the window, hears the engine warming up and the exterior hatch closing.

His little brother.

Richard snaps open the phone and speed dials. “Call the hospital. Let them know I'm on my way. I'll reroute directly to New Mexico. If you would like to meet Eddie, meet me there.”

Richard imagines seeing Eddie again, remembers the fury and dismay of their last conflict, remembers the kid he spent every minute of every day with for so many years. Paige is talking, but he hasn’t heard her. The plane starts to taxi and Richard buckles his seat belt.

“I have to hang up now Paige. We are taking off.”

* * *

The silver eagle rider that chased Eddie down is on a cell phone in a hospital corridor. This time he's wearing a dress shirt, tie and doctor's lab coat instead of black tactical gear. But his piercing blue eyes and snow white hair haven't changed at all.

“He's got two collapsed lungs, a broken pelvis, and a fractured skull,” he says tersely.

“I didn't tell you to kill him, Colonel.” The voice on the other end of the phone is arrogant, arch, and no matter how much he’s being paid the white-haired man thinks it’s too little if he has to deal with this ass. Nothing in this assignment has been as advertised, and Eddie Maxwell is in a hospital because he’s been underestimated from the start. “Did you tell him to go for a joy ride at 90 miles an hour in an RV built in 1971?”

“Has he said anything?” the voice demands.

“We are still waiting for him to regain consciousness, but we're set up to record whatever comes out of his mouth.”

“As soon as he's OK to transport, I want him out of there. I'll do some calling around to see where we can put him.”

“Well,” says the Colonel with a sigh. “That may be difficult. The hospital tells me his brother is on the way.”

CHAPTER 2

A black helicopter idles in the red dust of a New Mexican afternoon. It's rotors are blowing a cloud of thick sand off a helipad that sits atop a small community hospital. Richard steps out of the helicopter into the sun. He looks crisp in a dark grey suit and white shirt. He has a bluetooth device plugged into his ear and his tablet computer in his hands. He studies several pages of a virtual bank statement as he speaks to someone a thousand miles away from here.

"The transaction cleared a quarter of an hour ago. I'll move the resources into T-bills over night, then into the short term loan program," he shouts over the roar around him.

Richard's aide follows him out of the helicopter and walks past him, extending his hand to Paige who waits at the edge of the roof near the elevators. She is dressed as if for work, blond hair in a ponytail, tailored khaki suit, low-heeled boots. A camera swings from around her neck. As Richard approaches, she shouts to be heard.

"Eddie hasn't woken up!"

Richard holds up a hand to silence her. She stabs the elevator call button with her index finger.

"Long term I'm thinking of the Brazilian project. The one we already discussed. I have to get some new numbers from them. I'll send them over when I can!" Richard listens for a moment, then terminates the call.

He looks at Paige who is staring at him. The doors behind her open and she steps inside the metal box. Richard and the aide follow her in. Richard is surprised to see that Paige is furious and she has been crying.

"So glad you could join us," she says woodenly.

The elevator doors slide closed. When they emerge from the elevator doors and enter the hospital hall, Richard asks, "Why does this bother you so much?"

"That I've known you for a decade and you failed to mention a brother? You lied to me," Paige is so furious that she won't look at him. "You said you had no family."

"Because I don't," Richard replies. He is not the first person to write off a family member, or to be written off by one. A tremendous gulf suddenly stretches between them, and it's filled with a history he has done everything to put behind him. What matters is who he is now, the man he made himself, not the person he was born or the "family" he was born into.

"Well I hope you won't forget you have a wife as easily as you forgot you had a brother," Paige says as she leads him toward the ICU.

Richard, Paige and the Aide stop near a nurses' station outside a windowed I C U isolation room. A pair of nurses are in the area. A desk nurse is working on the station computer. Another nurse is filling in a chart on a clipboard.

In the isolation room, Eddie's head is in bandages, his face is badly bruised. There's a big tent that covers his lower body. Also inside the room there is a seventy-year old man who could pass for homeless. He is dressed in blue jeans and a long sleeved white shirt that's seen better days. He's wearing pointed alligator boots and a dirty straw hat.

"Richard turns to a Nurse who is filling in a chart. I'm Richard Maxwell here to see my brother, Eddie. I'd like some privacy. Can you clear the room?"

"Of course. Give me a moment."

Richard's phone rings as the woman enters the room

to speak to the old man. Richard answers the call and the desk nurse looks up.

“Yes. Move all of it into treasuries,” he says.

“You can't use that in here,” the nurse says firmly.

Richard turns away from her, pressing his free hand over his ear so he can hear. “Whatever rate you can get. We are looking at twenty-four hours. Maybe Forty-eight.”

The desk nurse rises. “Turn that off!” This time her words are sharp.

“I have to go.” Richard ends the call, puts his phone in his pocket and takes the earbud from his ear. He looks at the desk nurse. “You know there are no studies that show hospital equipment is affected by cell phone use. Not a single one.” He mentions this in a conversational tone because it’s not something that most people know. Cell phones can take down a plane, but hospital equipment has never been effected.

The nurse gives Richard a fierce look and returns to her seat. “Hospital staff and hospital patients are quite irritated by them however, so I'll have you removed if you use it again.”

Paige reaches into Richard's pocket and takes the phone. She hands it to the aide.

The door to the isolation room opens. The old man

exits, spies Richard and stops, apparently astonished. “Richard?”

The old man closes the distance between them. He is slightly taller, slightly broader, and heavier set, and he embraces Richard like a long lost son.

Paige and the aide both move so they can see Richard's face. He is clearly nonplussed by this warm welcome, but neither is he surprised by it.

“Hello Oscar.” Richard frees himself without being abrupt, then steps back to put some distance between himself and the old man who is somewhat inebriated and wiping away tears.

“I never thought I'd see you again. Eddie said you'd given him up.” The man has a south of the border accent, and he speaks of Eddie as though they have known one another for a lifetime.

Richard's looks startled, then stern. “Are you still working for Eddie?”

“Not for years. Three? Four? I told him he had to stop. I told him it was too dangerous. They will get him, just like they got your Dad. But, you know, he never listens. The sheriff called me when they couldn't find anyone else. Eddie bailed me out of the drunk tank a couple of times, so they had his number in my file.” Oscar reveals this as if it is the most natural thing in the world. He appears completely comfortable with Richard who seems anything but comfortable with him.

“Well, I'm very glad you were here for him. I should get in there. Why don't you give your contact information to my aide. Maybe we can talk later.” As the aide draws Oscar away, Richard enters the isolation room and shuts the door.

Paige positions herself so she can study both Richard and Eddie through the window.

Richard approaches his brother. He takes in the bandages around the head, the older but still familiar face, the mangled chest and the multiple IV bags hanging on the nearby metal stand. Eventually he reaches out to take his brother's hand. He remembers walking a little kid across the street, taking him to the bathroom, sitting next to him in a car. This is going to be much harder than he imagined.

“Jesus, Eddie, what have you gotten yourself into?”

A white haired man enters the room as he speaks. A lab coat, a clipboard, a stethoscope, a hospital ID, he examines the readings on several machines. He speaks to Richard without looking at him. “You're the brother, right? Richard Maxwell.”

“Yes.” Richard contemplates the clipboard and it strikes him as an anachronism. All the data on all the machines is digital, and the hospital is wired for wi-fi, so does anything really need to be recorded on paper anymore? If so, that's a problem sincerely in need of a solution.

"I'm going to ask you to step outside for a moment. We need to talk about your brother's condition," says the man, underlining one of the numbers on his page before looking up to meet Richard's eyes.

Richard, now in Richard's company, is disinclined to leave. Instead he wants answers. "How did the accident happen?"

"Single car accident on the interstate," replies the man with a sigh. "His blood alcohol was point one five."

Richard finds himself wondering who this is. A doctor? A hospital official. He has a stethoscope and a lab coat. But something about his manner is off. Also, something feels like a lie. Richard has learned to trust his instincts for a wide variety of reasons.

"I don't think Eddie drinks," he says. Which is an understatement because the Eddie he knew never ever drank. He wouldn't drink. Because he was a man on a mission to save the world and he was well aware that his mind was a Stradivarius, an instrument to be protected and used, not poisoned.

The man says, as if Richard has agreed to something, "We're currently arranging transport to Albuquerque."

“Is it safe to move him?”

“We don't have the facilities here to treat him, Mr. Maxwell. He needs surgery.”

Eddie's hand squeezes Richard's several times, and it is like a man coming back from the dead. Richard starts but does not look down. He works hard to keep his attention riveted on the man who has said several alarming things in just a few seconds. Eddie’s an alcoholic, needs to be moved, needs surgery, and is about to be transported.

“But are you sure it's safe to move him?” Richard asks again. Eddie’s hand is still convulsing, creating a staccato rhythm which sends cold fire through his veins. Suddenly he has the sense of being “back in the shit” again, a boy dealing with a demented little brother and a mad man’s problems.

“It's critical.” the man says firmly.

“I am afraid I'll need a second opinion,” replies Richard. This is a speeding train and it’s one he wants to get off. It’s one he wants Eddie off.

“We've already ordered the transport.”

“Without my consent?”

“We didn't think you'd make it in time.”

“Well I'm here now, I need a second opinion, and I

need some time alone with my brother."

"The arrangements have already been made, Mr. Maxwell. We have a team prepping."

Richard decides to make things simple. Clearly this person isn't interested in answering any questions so he serves less than no person at all. "My brother won't be moved without my consent. Now please leave the room or I'll sue you for malpractice."

The white haired man and Richard lock eyes for a long moment, and Richard wonders if he will have to call the police. Can one call the police from a hospital room?

To his relief his opponent leaves the room looking every inch the pissed-off medical man.
Eddie's hand continues to move and Richard looks around the room mystified. He spies a small electronic device attached to the steel rail of Eddie's bed. It appears to be a microphone. It's a bug but not a scorpion.

Richard slowly turns to look over his shoulder. Paige, the aide and Oscar are watching him with concern. The white haired man is behind them, speaking quickly as he steals glances at those assembled nearby. Richard turns back to Eddie whose hand movements have become frantic.

"There are no scorpions here Eddie. You're safe now. I promise," he says, wondering if the assurance he's given will sound anything but crazy to whoever is listening on that tiny electronic device. It occurs to him that bugging a hospital room is something that would only happen in Eddie's world, in their father's world. In the real world where Richard has lived forever so long, it's something that does not compute.

Eddie convulses, his eyes open wide, his head swivels to look at Richard in horror. Alarms sound.

A doctor in his sixties, a real one this time, races down the hall and into the room. Both ICU nurses join him. Richard looks out through the window. The white-haired man is gone, apparently not important enough to join the code blue party.

The new doctor looks at Richard.

"Who are you? What happened?"

"I am his brother. I already told the nurse. He opened his eyes and now he's having some kind of a seizure."

Richard steps out of the room as more doctors and nurses arrive to save Eddie's life. He motions to his aide. "Contact Davis at Cedars in Los Angeles. Get Eddie's medical records sent to him now. Tell Davis I want my brother airlifted there immediately. Make all the arrangements. I want Eddie out of here as soon as humanly possible."

"What's going on?" Paige asks.

"We're going to get Eddie to another hospital," Richard says firmly.

The aide, already on his phone, walks down the hall to get a better connection.

Richard hired the guy because he is a fully qualified mechanical engineer, with a second degree in economics, and he speaks fourteen languages. He earns two hundred and fifty thousand a year to follow Richard around and handle problems for him. He sees himself as Richard's apprentice and Richard thinks he might be. Today Richard will find out if he's really good at handling curve balls.

"Is it safe to move him?"

"I don't know. But Eddie is getting out of here."

A nurse exits Eddie's room, disappears into a floor pharmacy, returns with a pair of vials. She enters the room and hands the vials to the second nurse who fills two syringes and then injects the medication into Eddie's IV. His thrashing subsides.

Paige is clearly stunned by this suddenly very active interest in Eddie's well being. "Why?"

"Because he wants out of here," replies Richard. Paige has a soft heart and a keen mind and she will have many questions for him in the days and weeks to come. They will be questions he doesn't want to answer, has avoided answering, for a long time.

"How on earth do you know that? He's unconscious.

He has been since you got here.”.

Richard turns to look at her. He speaks softly. “Morse code.”

“What are you talking about?”

“We learned it as kids,” he replies. She seems eager to come to welcome Eddie into the family, wants to know everything, so why not start with the truth. His brother hasn’t been entirely unconscious and he and his brother are quite used to speaking in code. He wonders how much crazy she can take before she breaks.

The aide has returned and Richard turns to him. “Mister Maxwell the medical transport helicopter will be here in forty minutes.”

As the sun slides down behind the horizon, Richard's corporate helicopter hovers above a white medical transport chopper that rests on the now spot lit pad. While Richard, Paige and the pilot watch, Eddie's stretcher is brought up in the elevator by the white haired doctor and two bulky orderlies. Richard, seated behind the pilot and his aide, points at the ground.

“Get that helicopter on the radio!” Richard says as the men usher Eddie’s unconscious body across the tiny landing pad.

The pilot reaches for the handset.

“What's going on?” Paige asks. She is leaning forward to watch what’s happening.

“I don't want those men on Eddie's flight. We hired a crew. They came out with the chopper. They were just briefed by Dr. Davis at Cedars and Eddie's attending physician. We were waiting for them to bring Eddie up. This isn’t right.”

While they all watch, the doors on the chopper slide shut.

“I need to speak to that pilot,” says Richard sharply.

“He's not picking up,” the pilot replies.

Without warning, the helicopter below lifts off, darting forward low and fast across open country toward mountains that are perhaps twenty miles away.

Richard finds himself accepting the inevitable, slipping into a state of angry, frightened, and irritable acceptance he hasn’t known for a decade. “I knew this was going to be a circus. Follow them. Get the FAA on the radio. Let them know we have a hijacking.”

“You're kidding.” Paige is aghast. Richard finds himself wondering if her years in war zones will kick in now and she’ll more readily accept what she sees and hears.

"Watch. They won't follow the flight plan. I don't know what Eddie's involved in, but clearly someone will stop at nothing to have him," says Richard. The accident, the bug, the white-haired man, the kidnapping, it's all adding up to Eddie in big trouble, and maybe the kind of trouble even Richard can't get him out of.

Richard's helicopter races along behind the medivac helicopter which is now flying at high speed into the foothills.

"Damn, the FAA says they just lost their transponder," says the pilot.

"Tell them they have ours and we'll stay with the rogue flight," responds Richard.

"They are taking us into the canyons. That's dangerous flying. Especially at night."

"You're up to it, right?" Richard knows a military man when he sees one, and so many chopper pilots have combat experience.

The pilot smiles a little. "Two tours in the sandbox."

Richard's chopper picks up speed. Richard, Paige and the Aide all grab something to steady themselves. As the medical helicopter enters the canyons flying low and fast, its lights go out.

"They turned their lights off? Why would they do

that?" The dismay in Paige's voice is felt by everyone.

The Medivac plane dips, flies just above the brush.

"Hold on," says their pilot, dropping down to just above the brush line in pursuit.

The Medivac, navigating the ever darker maze of canyons, switches direction over and over again at the last second. The Pilot shakes his head.

"I have to back off. He's going too fast and flying too low. He's going to hit something."

And, as just predicted, one of the MediEvac's blade's does indeed strike a canyon wall hard. The copter now has three blades, none of them spinning, and tumbles from the sky. When it hits the ground like a broken dragonfly it explodes.

Eddie is only dimly aware of the fire consuming his helicopter. He is already heavily anesthetized after all. Looking up from within the wreckage he can see his brother's helicopter hanging overhead. He knows Richard will do whatever he can, but he already knows it won't be enough. It was worth it, Eddie thinks drunkenly, defiantly. Every minute of it. Every instant. Every single sacrifice. For even a chance at victory. Of course he has regrets, but he won't feel them for long. He won't feel anything for long because now he can feel the great engine of the world falling away.

* * *

Standing on the hillside next to the wreck, Richard grimly watches his brother's body extracted from the smouldering steel by firefighters and paramedics as Paige weeps beside him.

“Eddie Maxwell is dead.” At the top of the Canyon, a scorched and bedraggled Colonel looks down on them as he speaks into his cell phone. The two operatives he brought with him onto the chopper are nursing burns. The Colonel watches the wreckage being shifted by men with ropes, knows they are looking for more bodies, and he wonders what they’ll make of the young pilot with a bullet in his head.

“That’s impossible!” The rage the Colonel hears in the voice triggers nothing but irritation.

“My pilot didn't expect pursuit. You didn't tell me Richard Maxwell was also insane,” the Colonel says simply.

Lack of information, bad intel, that was always the cause of mission failure. When clients didn’t provide enough information, they didn’t get the services they paid for. As a mil ops commander now working stateside as a contractor, the Colonel was swiftly becoming used to clients who lied. One great thing about civilian wet work, he found himself thinking, is that one could actually quit a job.

CHAPTER 3

Richard is seated at a big desk in his luxurious home study. Paige is sleeping, fully clothed, on his couch. They arrived home just a few hours ago, exhausted, and he decided to check his email. She wanted to keep him company. The TV is on low. The room is dark. The walls around him are filled with the comforting presence of several thousand engineering books, all of which he has read.

Dozens of financial feeds on a monitor next to Richard dimly show data from markets around the world, but Richard is now flipping slowly through a large worn photo album. From time to time he glances at the feeds. When he does, some numbers swim and change colors. When this happens he reaches over, types something and the feeds change. He plays the markets like a video game.

The relic he holds features yellowing pictures and

sticky pages. It has the kind of photos you used to have to get developed at a store. It's almost an archaeological artifact at this point, but he's never recaptured the photos in the book with the phone on his camera because it's part of a past he wants to remain buried.

In one picture there's the RV Eddie destroyed in his accident. Richard and Eddie are boys of six and ten standing by a father whose hair has already gone gray. All three Maxwells have a steel-eyed stare that makes you think they take everything seriously.

In another picture the grey haired dad is lecturing a class of young men in uniform. He's drawn some complex machinery and equations on a chalkboard. There's something that looks like an antenna reaching up to touch long waves in the sky.

Richard unfolds an old newspaper article that's been thrust into the album. The photo in the article shows that a large explosion has ripped apart what looks like a barn. The headline is *TRAGIC ACCIDENT KILLS NINE*.

Richard turns the page to see himself graduating *magna cum laude* from MIT. He remembers the day, the sense of embarrassment and guilt that made him look down and away from the camera. No one else in his year had a chance. They had worked so hard to achieve what he had earned with no effort at all. It hardly seemed fair. But then, by then, he knew nothing was ever fair.

A final page, this one pulled from the CAL-Tech newspaper shows Eddie, smiling into the camera, as he accepts his own *magna cum laude* recognition. Eddie sees his success as everyone's success because he is determined to save the world.

Richard closes the book, stares at it for a moment, then sets it aside.

He looks back at the numbers sliding across the screen. Some flash in the characteristic way and he enters something on the keyboard. Almost all of the numbers turn green. A few thousand here, a few thousand there, occasionally it adds up to real money but never to anything more.

The next morning Richard, freshly showered and looking his completely in-control self, is back at work in his home office. His hands fly over his keyboard. The monitor is covered with hundreds of streaming and scrolling figures. In the lower right corner of the screen, his aide is talking.

"Did you send me those calculations I asked for? Do you have designs to match?" he asks the live feed.

"I believe you have them Sir. Please check your inbox," Andre replies. His aide has a name and Richard knows it. But when he works everyone is a component. A cog. It's easier that way. But today he finds himself thinking that Andre was with him when Eddie died. Andre had taken it upon himself to handle the collection of Eddie's remains, the cremation, and perhaps in a week or two Richard and Paige would set aside time for interment. That was something Richard couldn't face yet because he knew none of Eddie's friends, could legitimately accept none of their condolences or well wishes.

Richard clicks something on the keyboard and engineering drawings come up. He's looking at schematics for a hydro-electric power plant. Pages flip by. A buzzer interrupts his review.

"Harold Wilde on the phone," says Richard's telecommuting secretary.

"Let me call you back, Andre," says Richard as he drops the live feed.

"Transfer him," Richard tells the secretary.

"Richard. I was very sorry to hear about your brother," says the well known voice. Dr. Wilde is chairman of the board for Richard's investment company. He's also the biggest investor, the man who greenlights where the big money goes, and someone Richard turns to when he needs government hurdles removed.

"Thank you," says Richard formally, "We weren't close."

Dr. Wilde has always been slightly paternal, and Richard who has had enough of fathers, has always worked to keep things professional. Clear boundaries are good business when big money is involved.

“I think that probably makes losing him even harder. I am calling with some news that might be seen as a blessing. The board has decided you should take a leave of absence.” Dr. Wilde announces this in the same matter-of-fact way he might announce another ten million dollar equity investment or the need to liquidate thirty million in assets over the next three months.

“Why?” Richard keeps his voice level.

“Take some time to wrap up loose ends, vacation. When was the last time you took some time for yourself? Hasn't it been years?”

“What's going on?”

“Well, to be honest, this morning I received a heads up from the Justice Department that Eddie Maxwell was on the Domestic Terrorist list. Homeland Security seems to think he might have been working on some kind of weapon.” Wilde doesn’t sound surprised by this. It’s as if he has always known about Eddie, which Richard rather suspects he has. Richard is actively managing a fund worth upwards of a billion dollars. He knows he’s not entitled to any secrets. Then again, he knows that what he is hearing is entirely wrong.

“That's ridiculous. Eddie devoted his entire life to helping people,” he says firmly.

“Those two things aren't mutually exclusive,” Wilde points out.

“Well, frankly, I don't understand what this has to do with me,” replies Richard, letting go any notion of trying to defend a brother he has always found indefensible.

“In the current climate, while your family is under investigation, any transactions you are involved in will come under additional scrutiny. I am sure our lawyers can resolve the matter, but we need a few days to untangle the mess,” Wilde replies confidently.

Richard sits back in his chair and closes his eyes. “How long? A week?”

“More like two or three. We'll let you know when it's OK to come back.”

The call terminates and Richard listens to the dial tone.

* * *

Richard is seated at his huge dining room table in his huge sunny dining room. He is sweaty, dressed in running clothes, unshaven, morose, and bored. It's been less than twenty-four hours and he is already tired of his time off. He works because it's restful, because it's winnable, and because it's easy. What is this leisure notion people are always trying to foist off on others. Leisure means waiting around for something to happen.

Paige walks through the front door with the mail. She holds a four inch thick manilla envelope completely covered with one dollar postage stamps. There looks to be about two hundred dollars worth of postage on the thing and Richard eyes it warily.

Paige puts it on the table and slides it toward Richard. She watches him pick it up, turn it over, and sees him take in Eddie's name which is written on the back in black sharpie.

Richard slides it back to her. "Throw it away. There's nothing we can do for him now and it will be something insane."

Paige stares at him, picks up the package, and tears it open. She pulls out a thick pile of pages, each covered from corner to corner in hundreds of apparently random numbers.

She flips through the pages, trying to make sense of them.

"See? Something crazy just like I said."

Paige looks back inside the envelope, then dumps it out on the table. A brightly colored metal scorpion made of twisting triangles falls on it's back. It instantly rotates it's vertices until it is standing upright on eight sharp little feet. It is palm sized and its raised tail features a one inch black needle.

Richard eyes it and says, "Jesus. Even crazier than I expected. Thanks Eddie."

The words are harsh, but something in him leaps at this message from the grave.

The scorpion runs toward Richard as if it is voice activated and Richard stands up, thinking to himself that this is actually creepy. Eddie sent him a bug. A scorpion.

The scorpion is now on the end of the table apparently looking up at him. Except it has nothing that looks exactly like eyes. Unless maybe it's the little bars that look something like mandibles near what should be the thing's mouth.

"Is it a toy?" Paige asks?

Richard moves closer to the table and stares at the bug. He cautiously extends a hand and the scorpion swiftly scrambles onto it. Richard turns his hand over and the scorpion adjusts its position to remain on top.

“I think the scales are computer chips and it's got optical sensors that let it see,” he says, marveling at this jewel of a creature. How very Eddie to create a scorpion made of multi-colored metal chips. His brother’s manufactured animal moves exactly like a living thing. It’s sturdy and agile and it is smart enough to know who Richard is and what it wants.

Paige bends down to study the creature. She holds out her hand and Richard tries to drop the bug into it. Instead the little scorpion clings to Richard's hand.

As Paige moves to grasp it, the bug backs away from her touch by going up Richard's arm.

“My new digital friend,” he says wryly.

“I don't like the look of that tail,” she says suspiciously.

“Clearly it's for children three and over,” he replies.

Paige, still holding the pages, looks down at them. She holds them out to Richard.

“Now what's this?”

Richard takes the stack of pages, ignoring the bug as it climbs up his arm to avoid falling onto the floor. As he flips through the hundreds of sheets, numbers and letters become colors that flash and seethe. His mind struggles to make sense of what it sees.

After a moment he looks away. He weighs the document for a moment, then he walks to a trash can and drops it in. He stares down at it for a long time. His brother is dead and whatever that pile of trash has to say it won't bring Eddie back. Maybe he'll keep the bug but he's skipping whatever invitation that is.

"It's madness," he tells Paige. "You have no idea how insane Eddie could be. It wasn't all scorpions, sadly." He gives her astonished face a long look, taking in how much she loves him and how troubled she is by what appears to be his very hard heart. Explaining won't make things better because there is no explanation for Eddie.

Richard walks out of the living room into his study, his new friend gripping his shirt collar with tail and legs.

A football game is on the large format TV that dominates the room. Richard sits down on the couch to watch it. He finds sports mildly interesting, an almost predictable numerical series created over a season with team performance not quite governed by individual achievement. Sometimes the best team didn't have the best players. Thus the foundation of moneyball.

Paige comes into the room carrying the thick stack

of pages. She drops them on his desk, then comes to sit on the couch next to Richard. After a time her position shifts and she turns to look at the scorpion just a few inches away from her left ear. With a tentative finger she reaches out to touch it. It backs away, moving up Richard's neck.

"Actually, don't do that," says Richard, not liking the feeling of the bug on his skin and remembering the sharp point on it's tail.

Paige moves very fast, bringing her hand down on top of the scorpion in an attempt to snatch it up. She screams and jumps, falling off the couch and clutching her hand in pain.

The scorpion defiantly shifts back to a position on Richard's shoulder. What should be the thing's head is now pointed at her.

"It shocked me!"

She holds up her hand and there's a burn in the middle of her palm.

"That's quite a jolt from a little bug," says Richard with some surprise. He reaches up to collect the creature and turns it over so he can examine its underside. It's legs wriggle in defiance.

"I wonder what it runs on."

"Who would make something like that?" asks Paige in dismay.

"A fellow with advanced degrees in electrical and mechanical engineering. A PHD in applied science. And way too much time on his hands. For some reason Eddie probably thought this would persuade me to wade through that," says Richard.

He nods at the pages on his desk.

"Well what are you going to do with that thing? We can't keep it around if it's going to sting people. Especially if those people are me."

"I don't know," says Richard thoughtfully. "Maybe it will go to sleep."

The scorpion folds itself up into a cube and drops into Richard's lap. He picks it up and examines it from every angle. It's a fully self-contained unit that looks like nothing more than a multicolored die that lacks the spots required to play a game.

"Wake up?" he says, and watches as the scorpion unpacks itself.

"Go to sleep," he says once more. The scorpion folds up again and Richard rises to place it atop the pages Eddie sent. He looks at Paige, noticing that she is staring at her hand.

"My family is chock full of unpleasant surprises," he says, thinking of the many times he has seen something go from wonderful to appalling in a matter of seconds.

Paige watches Richard return to his seat on the couch and she moves to sit next to him. He wraps his arm around her and pulls her close. She settles herself against him in a position that lets her stare at the scorpion cube.

* * *

Richard is seated at his desk again. Page is asleep on the couch in her pajamas, her laptop beside her, a blanket covering her feet. She fell asleep waiting for him to come to bed which is something he never quite got around to. This is a common theme in their married life. This house in the Hamptons has over a dozen rooms, but they live in four for the most part, and most of the time is spent in this windowless study.

Richard moves the scorpion cube to the center of his desk. He picks up Eddie's document and starts flipping through it. Page after page goes by and to Richard it seems colors begin to wash over them in every shade of electric illumination. After a couple of passes he realizes some pages are light brown, some dark brown, some green, some black.

Richard weighs the pile for a moment, shakes his head ruefully, then rises. He walks into the dining room.

Paige, the blanket pulled around her, comes into the dining room the next morning to find the long table moved aside and Richard on his hands and knees positioning pages corner to corner on the floor.

“What is it?”

Richard looks up.

“An image map.”

“You mean a picture?”

Richard nods.

“But it's all letters and numbers.”

“Pixels.”

“How many colors?”

“Sixty Four.” Richard takes a piece of tape and connects two more corners.

“What's it a picture of?”

“I already said. It's a map.”

Paige steps forward, looks down.

“Oh. An actual map. Of a place. I thought it was a code.”

Richard smiles.

“It is.”

Richard reaches the end of a row, stands up, stretches his back. “I need coffee.”

Having moved into the state of the art kitchen, Richard puts water in the kettle and then puts the kettle on the stove. Paige sits in a chair as he grinds coffee for the french press.

“How did you figure that out so fast?”

“You know that when I see numbers I see colors. Well, Eddie did too. Every family shares something. We shared synesthesia.”

“That number and color thing never made sense to me. Numbers aren’t colors, their pictures.”

Richard seats himself in a chair once the water is brewing in the grounds. “What color is Monday?”

“I don't know. Blue?”

“Tuesday?”

“Maybe Yellow?”

“So what’s three?”

“I don't know.”

“But you know what colors days of the week are.”

“Blue Mondays. There's a song.”

“Is there a yellow Tuesdays song?” Richard asks curiously.

When she doesn't reply he pours the coffee, contemplating a past he has never wanted to talk about as he collects milk and sugar and cups to complete the coffee ritual they have begun.

"Mom was a mathematician. PHD. Brilliant. Dad, an engineer. Military initially, nuclear then high frequency electrical projects. Eddie and I were freaks born to freaks. Synesthesia is the mapping of one sense on to another. He and I, like my Mom, could see numbers as colors. Random numbers look like colored dots, but meaningful sequences of numbers look like colored streaks and steps and curves. Important numbers pop out. It's a kind of high functioning autism I believe."

"That sounds like a drug trip," she replies as he pours coffee in her cup.

"That's why I'm comfortable with markets. I'm not seeing the numbers, I'm seeing waves of colors. If I look hard I can make out individual numbers, but my brain automatically tries to see numerals as part of a pattern. So I see trends others miss. It's just a trick of the mind. Eddie sent me a message only I could read."

"And a toxic little toy," she adds. "He seems amazing. I mean it seems as if he must have been."

Richard nods. "He was. And incredibly, fanatically,

impractical to the point that it was actually terrifying. So I am going to read his message in a bottle because there's no reason not to and he did a lot to get it to me. But that's as far as this will go."

Richard and Paige share their coffee in silence, then Richard says, "Hurry up and get dressed. We have lots to do."

* * *

Paige is kneeling on the floor using a marker to paint a sea of numbers brown. In the middle of the numbers she sees a collection of 64s. She colors them black creating a solid rectangle.
She stands up, looks down, then backs up as she tries to take in the whole picture at once.

Richard, having finished his corner of the pictures, joins her and together they study the map which seems to show a large flat mesa bordered on one side by a cliff. Black lines run all the way across the map from the bottom to the top.

"What are those white spots up there in the corner?"

"Latitude and Longitude in hexadecimal I think."

"Is that yellow thing a road?"

"Let's find out."

Richard collects his tablet from the study and returns to the dining room. He enters the coordinates and then stares at the floor a little longer. "My brother literally sent me a map to the middle of nowhere in Arizona. Isn't that odd?"

"We should go," she says. "We've got nothing else to do. Why not?"

"The government says he was a domestic terrorist," replies Richard. He knows that it's a mistake to go wherever this map wants to take them, but that scorpion and these pages are so compelling. This is like having his brother back. And really, what harm can it do? Eddie is dead. Whoever tried to kidnap him knows he's dead. This is just a long drive to nowhere and there's no reason not to take it.

"But you know Eddie wasn't a terrorist and you saw him murdered," says Paige.

"That is true," he replies.

There's probably nothing much where they are going. But Eddie was murdered and he did send this message and something in Richard rebels at the idea of not knowing what it's all about.

"So I'll go pack and we'll go see whatever it was he wanted to show you," says Paige as if it's all been decided.

"I guess I better fold up the map," he replies. It seems

smart to take this awkward document with them. Maybe it has more clues he hasn't found. Maybe it's just the kind of thing that shouldn't be left behind for others to look at. In any case, it is the map his brother gave him and he wants it.

"I'll see you in the car in ten." Paige says.

She knows everything about packing light and getting places fast. Her work takes her all over the world at a moment's notice. She is drawn from tragedy to horror, from triumph to sacrifice, for news agencies who need the million dollar photos that win hearts and change minds.

Soon she hopes to have a picture of who her husband truly is.

CHAPTER 4

Richard and Paige, both in sunglasses, and dressed in the kind of casual wear that looks good on safari, bump down a dirt road in an expensive sports car.

Above them massive electrical pylons look like a long row of iron men holding power cables over their heads. In the middle of this arid plateau, a hundred feet from one of the metal giants, and a hundred feet below the dozens of cables it carries, there is an old wood shack.

Richard and Paige race toward it.

* * *

Dr. Wilde, 70, white-haired, portly, and grandfatherly, is dressed in a white lab coat. He's seated in an expensive chair, at an expensive desk, in a spacious office that features floor to ceiling windows covered by thick curtains that offer him some privacy in what amounts to an expensive fishbowl. His computer screen shows a satellite picture of the sports car, the pylons, and the shack. He is speaking to Colonel White on speaker phone.

“Arizona? Why didn’t we know Eddie had a lab there?”

“It's just not in our files,” replies White. “He’s only been under full surveillance for about a year.”

“Well get down there. Check out the site. Bring Richard and his girlfriend back. I want to know how they knew something that we didn't.”

“I'm on my way.”

“How long?”

“We can be on site in four hours. Maybe six.”

“That's ridiculous. Why so long?”

“You want them alive? If you want them dead, I can just helo in a sniper. If you want them alive, I'll need a couple of dozen guys in case they run. Also I need state police support to close the roads and pick them up if they get around us. Sadly, all that takes a few hours to set up.”

“Let's avoid all police involvement,” replies Wilde.

“Then I'll need to hire even more men,” says the Colonel.

“Fine, but don't screw this up like you did the brother.”

“I can't stop people from killing themselves Doctor. Eddie did not want to be taken alive,” the Colonel replies coldly.

Eddie, the pilot, that’s two bodies. And the two of his guys injured in the helicopter. He doesn’t like how this job is going and he is disinclined to take any more chances by underestimating a Maxwell.

* * *

Richard and Paige step out of the car and stare at the structure they have driven more than a thousand miles to see. It looks to be nothing more than a shed. It has a porch but no windows. Just old wood walls, a battered door, and a shale roof that looks likely to leak.

“That was a big map for such a little building,” notes Paige.

Richard steps onto the dilapidated porch, walks to the door, and tries the handle. It turns. Richard and Paige enter the little cabin and look around. In one room there's an iron cot, an electric coffee pot and a hot plate.

A half open door shows an awkwardly placed toilet crammed up against a sink that sits under a broken mirror. Richard tries the faucet but not even a drop of water trickles out.

He leaves the bathroom and walks five steps to another door. He opens it to find a tiny back room. The walls and ceiling of this windowless closet are covered with newsprint, thumb tacks, black lines, red thread, and red writing. There are stacks of yellowed drawings everywhere including the floor.

Paige moves in to inspect the posted news articles which have headlines like *UFO SIGHTED OVER SEATTLE*, *DEATH RAY SHOOTS DOWN PLANE*, *CROP CIRCLES EXPLAINED*. She has stepped into a mad man's mind.

Richard shakes his head, turns around, and walks back out the front door. Moments later Paige joins Richard who is now sitting on the porch. She takes her place beside him and together they study the desert and scrub brush that shimmer in the late afternoon heat.

“I wonder why I'm here. I never wanted Eddie's insanity to be part of my life when he was alive. Why would I want it now that he's dead?”

“Why didn't you tell me about him? And don't give

me that crap that you didn't speak."

"But we didn't. Not for a very, very long time."

Paige says nothing.

Richard is surprised by the ache in his chest. The intense feeling of mystified loss. It had been a matter of morality, of sanity, of intellectual honesty that had set him apart from Eddie. He had never stopped caring about, even loving, his little brother. It was his love and admiration for Eddie that had eventually sawed them apart. Had he done wrong? Had there been another way?

"I'm remembering him," he says. "Eddie was brilliant. So facile. Such a lateral thinker."

Richard wonders if there is something wrong with talking about Eddie's mind and how brilliant he was. Is that the only measure of a man that matters to him?

"He was like you," says Paige.

Richard shakes his head ruefully. "No. Compared to Eddie I have always been a second class thinker. I'm very rigid. I want the right answer and I always think there's only one. But Eddie came up with answers to questions I never even thought to ask. That no one ever asked. He would tell me, even when we were very young, that there's an infinite set of right answers and I could see them all if I would just stop looking for only one."

Richard reaches into his pocket, pulls out the cube, and holds it in the palm of his hand. "I do not know what question this is the answer to, and that is beginning to bug me."

After a long moment he continues, "My Dad was a lead engineer on a successor to the Manhattan project. He was working to take nukes into space in order to power exploration. But his work got moved over to the military a few months after my mother died. He lost faith in himself, his country, and humanity all in one year."

"He had to know what he was building and what kind of men he was working for," replies Paige.

Richard shakes his head. "Dad and his friends were naive enough to see their work as an engineering problem. They assumed everyone shared their vision. Finding out they were wrong hit hard. Dad became obsessed with terrestrial power plants. He wanted to build something that didn't require uranium or plutonium. Something that actually helped people. Something even the poorest countries could own and no one could stop them from having. He came up with a design and tried to execute what should have been a trillion dollar project on the cheap, moving from place to place around the country, working with underground teams of lunatics just like him."

"Where were you while all this was going on?" Paige asks.

"Since our mother had died, and we had no one else, Dad took Eddie and I along for the ride. He gave us his version of an education, one filled with nothing but numbers, physics, and hard facts no one could deny. Our history books talked about inventions. Our english books were biographies about engineers. And Dad was rigorous. We worked hour after hour at learning everything he thought we should know. So much so that we taught one another cyphers and codes so we could talk about other things without being heard."

"So what went wrong? You never talk about your father. I've asked a hundred times."

"One day, there's an explosion. A fire. Nine people die including my Dad. I was thirteen, Eddie was nine. We became wards of the state. Needless to say we got into college. I started at sixteen. He started a year younger. We were always at odds after the accident so we went to different schools, chose to live entirely different lives," replies Richard.

"Your brother wanted to continue your Dad's work," says Paige.

"My brother would never make a weapon," says Richard, firmly. Remembering the hundred and one arguments that had escalated to a permanent separation, he simply could not believe that his brother's entirely altruistic and aggressively humanistic soul could ever become warped enough to mechanize death. It just isn't possible. "It was antithetical to everything he was. Everything Eddie stood for. I want to know who is lying about him and why."

Richard rises, slips the cube into his pocket, and walks back into the shack.

Paige sits a moment longer, then goes to the car, pops the trunk, pulls out a pair of sleeping bags, and walks back into the house. There are a lot of answers she means to have too.

* * *

Hours later Richard and Paige are sleeping. She is on the narrow cot. He is on the floor. All the papers from the back room are scattered around them because they have been read over and over again.

Metal scrapes against metal and Richard's eyes fly open. He has gone from deeply asleep to entirely awake so suddenly he is not sure that he isn't dreaming. He watches Paige sit up as the strange hollow metal sound comes again.

Then, from the bathroom a shape emerges. Large, misshapen, shuffling, with twin lights where eyes should be. Nothing could look more alien or be more unexpected in this little hovel, and suddenly all those news stories about aliens and spaceships come clearly to mind. Has Eddie created some kind of cosmic connection to people from another planet or another dimension?

The light flicks on.

Oscar, looking just as homeless as he did days ago, has his hand on a switch which resides on the wall just outside the bathroom. He is wearing a yellow construction hat that features bright high intensity halogen lamps. He's dressed in green coveralls which are coated in dust and old paint stains. When Oscar looks from Paige to Richard, Richard is all but blinded.

Richard raises a hand to shield his eyes and struggles to his feet in self defense.

"I heard someone up here. Thought it might be you," says Oscar in a now comfortingly familiar accent.

"What are you doing here?" Paige is now standing as well, her expression surprisingly placid for someone who has seen a bum appear from literally out of nowhere.

Richard walks past Oscar to look into the bathroom. He sees that the wall the mirror and sink are mounted to is actually a thick door. That explains why the faucet didn't work. The room now opens onto a stairway that leads down into absolute darkness.

“I camp out here when I'm low on cash. It's dry and there's a bunch of food stockpiled. Eddie didn't mind.”

“You heard us?” Paige asks. “From where.”

“Downstairs.” Oscar moves back into the bathroom, through the door, and out onto the stairs. Richard and Paige follow him, mystified. They find themselves standing on a small metal platform, something that might be part of a cat walk, and there are stairs that descend into darkness.

“Watch your step. It's a long way down,” suggests Oscar.

He reaches past them to close the door, and suddenly there is no light in the world except that on his head. He turns and leads the way down. Richard and Paige, startled to find they have embarked on this mission, follow him. They are unpleasantly surprised to discover that the stairs shiver and shake with every single step, and this odd scaffolding is suspended from the ceiling not connected to the ground.

“The staircase is shaking,” says Richard after a time.

“Polymer plastic. Sturdy, non-conductive, but more give than steel. Perfectly safe. At least for one person. I never tried three. Maybe we should spread out a bit to relieve stress on the joints," says Oscar.

His accent is as strong as ever, but somehow Oscar seems to be in his element here. Richard suddenly finds himself wondering if he has been played.

He dimly remembers Oscar as a younger man, someone who worked for his father. An engineer perhaps? Almost everyone had been. But a mexican-american engineer would have been such an anachronism in those days, especially one who dressed and spoke as Oscar did. Then again, maybe it made sense to hide in plain sight when you worked with crazy people, or maybe Oscar really was an intermittent drunk with a talent for prototype manufacture. One could be highly skilled and occasionally over imbibe from time to time.

Richard, Paige, and Oscar have moved farther apart, and Oscar is looking down at the steps so they all know where to put their feet when their turn comes.

"I think the biggest risk is slipping under the rail," offers Oscar helpfully. "It is not really OSHA compliant." He pauses to look at the rail and the light shows the wide gap any of them could fall through should they trip and fall.

Thereafter Paige clutches both rails like they are lifelines. Richard follows her, ready to make sure she doesn't fall away like Eddie did.

"I think you should have all this stuff ripped out,

now that Eddie is gone. The copper is worth a lot. You can sell it for scrap. Do you want me to help you?" Oscar is talking about something but Richard has no idea what it is?

"How much farther?" Paige asks.

Oscar turns to look up at her, and as he does his headlamps sweep the space around them. Something horrifying is illuminated for a split second. Something very big, very black, with hundreds of arms.

"Are you getting tired?" he asks curiously.

"Oscar, look to your left," says Richard.

Oscar obligingly looks off the side of the staircase. Richard is staring at a very large, very ugly, industrial explosion frozen in time. Long, arm-thick, black cables whip around them in every direction. A few have cracked to show a bright red copper core. Far off, at the center of what looks like a nest, something insectoid juts up. It appears to be several stories tall. Near them a pair of wires have split wide and the fragments look like snapping hydra heads.

"Jesus," says Paige.

Oscar looks down, apparently unaware that his lights have illuminated anything that might cause anyone any kind of concern.

"I think it's another 200 feet? Twenty stories? Maybe a little more," he says. Then he continues walking down.

Paige watches him a moment, then sits down on a step, clutching the rails to steady herself.

“Oh boy. I don't think I can do this,”

The stairway shivers and Oscar's lamp moves farther away.

Richard pulls out his phone, presses a button. It emits as much light as a flashlight. He focuses it on the steps and says, “Yes you can. We need to get down. Just focus on the steps. Don't worry about anything else.”

“Your brother was so crazy,” she says.

“Yes,” says Richard with a guilty sense of satisfaction, “Yes he was.” He finds himself thinking that it is easy to romanticize a dead Eddie who offers clever gifts like giant maps and pretty bugs. But this was the real Eddie, the Eddie that would stop at nothing.

Paige and Richard eventually exit the huge cylindrical shaft through which the stairs cut through a steel screen door that looks like it belongs in a prison or mine. They follow a short flight of rubber steps into a control room which is covered by a metal mesh that separates physically from the chamber they were just in while still allowing them to see up into it’s darkness.

The light on Oscar's mining hat now illuminates control panels, banks of electrical meters, and a 10 foot sliding steel door that opens into a rock corridor. Richard gestures at the madness above them.

“When did all that happen?”

“A few years back. Around when he said he didn’t need me anymore,” says Oscar.

“Was anyone killed this time?” Richard is almost afraid to know the answer. The machine in the multi-story rubber-lined cylinder they’d just passed through was a monster that had haunted him since the disaster that had turned him into an orphan.

“Reinforced concrete walls contained it. There was a fire, but extinguishers put it out. Not so bad.” Oscar shrugs off the disaster as if it is of no consequence. Just the remains of an experiment that didn’t work out.

A fluorescent light over a workbench is now flickering on. A second one follows suit a moment later. As Richard, Oscar and Paige, look around, all the lights come up in the control room.

Richard notices that the equipment in the room is dusty, black, antiquated. There is a panel of big circuit breakers along one wall. They are all thrown to off.

“Voice activated. You must sound like Eddie,” says

Oscar. "I have to use the switches."

"Richard!" clutches at his arm and even as she is backing away from a blocky metal six-legged insect, about the size of a cat, that's entered the chamber through the door to the rock corridor. Its spine appears to be a long metal rod. It has two prehensile metal "hands" near where its mouth should be, though it doesn't have a mouth to stuff things into. The creature moves stiffly, as if it thinks very slowly and needs lots of oil.

Oscar turns to Richard. "That's Spot."

"There's another one!" Paige points at a shoebox sized bug that has entered the control room through the metal door they just used. This one is faster and it's walking on the ceiling, metal hooks engaging with the mesh one step at a time.

"Sheila must have crawled in while I was hiking up," says Oscar.

Sheila, smaller and faster than Spot, makes her way down the walls to stand on the floor. She has a camera lens where a face should be, and all eight of her little feet can grip.

"Stop," says Oscar, and at his order the bug stops. He reaches down to scoop it up, then hands it to Richard. "This is prototype nine."

"Where are the other eight?" Paige is looking around

the room with some concern as Richard explores the bug in his hands.

“You and Eddie built all this?” Richard asks, nodding to indicate everything around them including the bugs.

“Used to be we had lots of guys. Back then we had lots of funding. When the money dried up they all had to go. Eddie kept me until last,” Oscar sounds a little proud of that. Claiming a friendship and an intimacy with a person he values. “He still used the lab sometimes. At least, I think so. He didn’t want to take it apart.”

Paige loosens her grip on Richard and walks toward an ancient computer system embedded in one of the control consoles. She pushes a key on a keyboard and it flickers to life. A password screen pops up. “What do I type?” she asks.

“Harvester,” says Oscar.

She enters the characters, but the computer only beeps and flashes, "No connection.”

“Eddie never kept his data here. It was always kept off site. You need the internet to login,” says Oscar.

Richard looks up at the dark chamber above them. He is trying to see through the mesh to the machine that failed. Is there something different about this iteration of his father’s device? Is this what Eddie wanted him to see? "Is there a way to turn on lights in there?"

As he asks the question, sounds of movement come from far above them. Steps that echo loosen dirt that sounds like rain. Then there is banging, as if someone is trying to break something.

"Did you bring anyone with you?" Oscar asks.

"No. I don't know who's up there, but I'd be willing to bet they aren't friendly," Richard is thinking of his brother's body last scene broken by the long fall in the chopper and burned by the resultant fire.

"We need to go," says Oscar. "It will take them a few minutes to figure out what's going on. And then-"

There's a huge explosion and a ton of rubble and rubber rain down. Richard now sees the starlit sky and moving lights high above them. A moment later, some of the lights start a slow descent, falling straight down like bright blue stars.

Each light is a man on a cable, and as they fall their lights illuminate the catastrophic still life of thick copper cable and a multi-story ant-like shape at the center of the disaster. Half of the would-be ant's head is gone, and one of it's six slender arms is blown off.

Richard moves to close the steel door between the chamber and the control room.

"Is there a way to lock this gate? We have to stop

them from getting down here," he tells Oscar.

Oscar walks over to the circuit breakers, One by one he starts switching them on. This triggers a hum so loud and low it echoes in the heart. Above them all rivers of electrical light start running along the massive broken cables, and the ant-like figure becomes more visible in the manufactured lightning. The beast starts to shift its position, angling itself for some purpose only it understands. The wires around it begin to wave, caught in powerful magnetic ripples the human eye isn't equipped to see. The explosion stopped years ago is beginning again. Oscar looks at Richard and Paige.

"Now, we should go."

Richard is aghast. "What did you just do?"

Inside the cylinder a dull blue glow is growing, and the hum is becoming a pounding pulse that shakes the walls. The wires inside the cage are twisting as if looking for something. The half dozen men on ropes inside the cage have stopped their descent and are now looking everywhere for a way out. There is only up and it won't be an easy climb to get there.

"This won't be pretty," remarks Osar without concern.

The wires start to whip with greater and greater speed, flying as the machine begins to churn.

“We aren't safe here!” says Oscar, reaching out to take Paige's arm. “We need to run!”

The machine inside the silo is now writhing wildly, cables are flying, and one whips hard on the screen that protects them, cutting into it and folding the metal mesh in.

Richard turns and follows Oscar and Paige into the tunnel. The mechanical repair insects attracted to him exit as well.

A coil of wire rips through the control room, the lights go out, and the hum has become a pulse that shakes the stone around them.

Oscar, Paige and Richard run up the tunnel past stockpiles of food, broken equipment, long coils of wire. The only illumination comes from the disaster going on behind them and Oscar's headlamps.

The ground is littered with pieces of metal, tools, and chunks of rock. The heavy pulse beats through the facility with increasing speed and strength, each beat louder and harder than the last.

Paige trips over a bar and falls hard on one knee.

Oscar, who has been pulling her forward, helps her up.

Richard looks back toward the explosion. In the flashes he sees an attacker has made it through Eddie's chamber of horrors into the tunnel. He has a wand with an electric blue tip in his hand. Some kind of taser or cattle prod?

Richard steps into the darkness and kneels near a giant spool of insulated electrical wire.

When the attacker races past, Richard throws himself into the man's side, hurling him hard to the ground. The wand goes flying. The battle instantly becomes a hand to hand fight which Richard swiftly finds he is losing. Richard snatches at the man's face, looking for an eye to gouge or a nose to break. His fingers find a mask and he jerks on it hard.

White hair, bright blue eyes. The "doctor" from the hospital, the man who murdered his brother, is suddenly before him.

Pinned to the ground, this demon on his chest, Richard's hands are scrabbling in the dirt, looking for purchase. His fingers come across something. A handle, something sharp. Without thinking he jams the rusty screwdriver into his attacker's side, plunging it in as far as it will go.

The man spasms in agony and Richard throws him off. Stumbling to his feet, Richard runs down the hall, following the merest hint of light, praying he can find Oscar and Paige before the cave collapses around him.

Richard finds himself barreling out into the Arizona

moonlight. An ancient green truck sits just outside the thick steel doors that must normally seal the access tunnel. The vehicle is already running, so Richard jumps in the truck bed and the vehicle sets out along a cliff side road that leads to the top of the mesa.

The ground shakes hard with every pulse, and as the old truck reaches the top of the mesa Richard can see the huge power pylon bending toward a gaping hole where Eddie's shack used to be.

Out of the hole black wires are reaching up, wrapping themselves around the electric cables the pylon holds. Long tendrils of lightning strike the pylon, the cables, the remains of Richard's car and the half dozen black utility vehicles parked nearby.

Men in black are running away from the maw across the moonlit desert plain.

Richard settles back in the truck bed to watch his father's monster work.

* * *

As the sky begins to lighten in the east, it is possible to see that Eddie's machine, the power pylon, and the power cables have fused into a twisted, burning, mass. All the cars nearby are overturned scorched hulks and there's a helicopter flying overhead.

“We didn't destroy the device. Maxwell did!” Major White is on the phone. He is sitting, half dressed, near one of the burned out vehicles. One of his men is strapping a bandage into place over the puncture wound in his side.

“Half the men we hired are dead, Doctor. Most of the western United States has lost power. So if you want Maxwell picked up fast, I can just put in a call to Homeland Security.”

“I need him brought to the lab, Colonel, not stuffed in a federal prison. If I’d wanted that I could make the call myself,” replies Dr. Wilde.

“Exactly. So I guess your only option is to focus your attention on your job, Doctor, while you leave me to attend to mine.”

* * *

Hours later, Wilde is in his office staring out the window at northern lights that paint the sky every color of blue and green. He addresses his speaker phone. “Our systems are fully functional. Power is being generated from the earth's electrical field as promised.”

“Your most recent report says there's a net energy loss,” says the General on the phone.

"In our recent tests we've been producing just over unity," corrects Wilde.

"I find that very hard to believe," says the second General on the phone. "In fact I would have to see it to believe it."

Wilde finds himself furious yet again. This fat general and his gaunt twin are on a two-man mission to clean up wasteful military spending, and Eddie Maxwell's refusal to make good on his promises have turned Wilde and this facility into a cherry apparently ripe for the picking.

And yet, a breakthrough is so close Wilde can taste it. He can produce power over unity. In fact once his units began producing power they are very hard to stop. There seemed to be a regulation system, some kind of throttle, required, some missing piece Eddie had created before he died to solve the specific problem he was facing now.

"Of course. I am happy to arrange a short demonstration. But I should warn you that we do have a problem with overheating that we are working to track down."

"Doctor, you are more than three years late delivering on a half billion dollar project, and you've made almost no measurable progress in the last eighteen months. Why should we believe you're anything but a fraud?"

Wilde lets a tiny percentage of the anger he's feeling creep into his tone. "By the end of the year I guarantee we'll meet all the contract requirements."

"No. That's not going to work this time," says the gaunt General, the one with four stars, "We'll be on site in a week. You will give us what we've paid for by then or we will ensure you go to jail. Are we clear?"

CHAPTER 5

Sitting in a small greasy spoon diner at a truck stop fifty miles from what used to be Eddie's lab, Paige, Oscar and Richard are dirty, tired, and morose.

Milk and pie remains litter a table illuminated by a candle and wan blue light coming through a picture window. A waitress in a 50's style pink and white uniform approaches. "Can I get you anything else? Some ice cream? Since the lights went out it's only a dollar."

"I think we're good," says Richard. "What's the damage?"

The waitress eyes the table. "I'd say twenty-five."

Richard offers her four tens and says "Keep the change. I'm sorry we've been here so long."

"Stay as long as you like. The breakfast crowd isn't

due for hours."

The waitress moves away and Richard tries to imagine where the breakfast crowd will come from when there isn't a town for miles. Highway traffic? Truckers who have been driving all night?

"What the hell just happened?" Paige asks. "I know those men were the people who killed Eddie, and I know they wanted to get us. But what did I just see?"

"I turned the Harvester on and it picked up where it left off," says Oscar.

When he fails to continue, Paige prods him. "When it's not ripping apart the world, what exactly does Eddie's machine do?"

"It makes power," says Richard.

"You mean it collects power," corrects Oscar.

"So you aren't sure either? Are we absolutely certain it's not a bomb?"

"Of course not. Eddie would never make a bomb. That's a harvester. It is supposed to harvest the ambient electricity generated by the earth's magnetic field," says Richard.
When Paige looks no happier, he continues.

"Here is the world's quickest course in electric generators. To make electricity you spin magnets around a conductor. A turbine in a dam is just a water-wheel that pushes magnets around and around a copper wire. That produces the kind of electricity that turns your lights on. The earth has a conductive molten iron core. The mantle of the earth spins around it at a thousand miles an hour. So the earth generates lots of electricity all the time. That machine tries to harvest it."

"The earth produces electricity?" Paige asks. This is something that she has never heard before.

"Where do you think lightning comes from?" Richard asks.

"Well, then Eddie's machine sounds pretty useful," Paige replies.

"It would be, if it worked. Which it never will." Richard

"I think it does work," says Oscar. "Eddie said that machine works like a tuning fork. You use a small amount of electricity to make it generate a magnetic field that's in resonance with the planet. Once it is in resonance, it starts collecting power very quickly. But there's no off switch except to discharge the energy in a "spark" or siphon the power off to a battery or capacitor. It flies apart if it can't discharge. That's what happened back there. There was nowhere for the power to go except to the pylon."

"Eddie rebuilt exactly the machine that killed Dad," says Richard. "I can't believe he took the risk."

"Maybe your dad and the other guys got the tuning right, and the energy had nowhere to go. When it blew up there was no containment so they were killed. Eddie created containment."

"All this misery for just another generator?" Paige asks. "It seems strange to invest a whole life, multiple lives, creating that."

"A brand new power source. If that machine worked, it would generate unlimited power whenever and wherever you want it," says Richard.

"And that's worth killing for?"

"You could operate one in downtown Manhattan and run the city forever. You could operate it in the middle of the Gobi desert to pump clean water in. Its clean infinite power anywhere it needs to be. No more oil, no more fracking. Eddie's machine would change the world," says Oscar. Seated in the candle-lit restaurant it's clear that Oscar is every inch an engineer who shared Eddie's lofty vision.

"Kind of a shame they always blow up," says Richard.

They climb back in the truck, Paige in the center, and Oscar starts the car. He pulls out on the main highway and starts driving into the sun.

"Where to now?" he asks.

"I need to get home. I have a magazine assignment

due Monday," says Paige.

Oscar looks at her, then over her head at Richard.

"Paige, our car was next to the shack. They know we were there. That guy who attacked me. He knows we made it out. If we go home, they'll arrest us," he says.

"Should we just turn ourselves in? Maybe the police can help us," she says.

"The government thinks Eddie is a domestic terrorist. I think if we turn ourselves in it will be a very long time before they let us go," says Richard. "We'll have to start by explaining what created that great big hole and why seven states don't have power."

Richard shakes his head. "No. We need to know exactly what Eddie was working on. We can use that as a bargaining chip. I just don't know how we're doing to find that out."

Oscar, driving, settles back in his seat. "Maybe this is the one weekend a year when I can find someone who knows exactly what Eddie was working on." He reaches the highway and follows a sign to Las Vegas.

* * *

Paige, Oscar and Richard ride up an escalator under signs that indicate they are at the International Weird Science Expo. At the top of the escalator a flurry of freaks and whackos, some in costume, some carrying boxes of junk, stand in line to get in.

Lining the floor of the lobby there are twenty or thirty narrow booths and tables covered in equipment, books, CDs, and DVDs. Working UFO toys are being guided over the crowd by some teenagers, while others are actively recruiting people for Star-Fleet and the Jedi Council.

Richard hears the usual nonsense go buy from the wingnuts and nerds that populate every conference.

“Don't forget the Madrid incident.”

“That could have been a manufactured mirage.”

“Chicago was more convincing.”

“The new T.I.A. program doesn't work like that. It tracks everyone all the time.”

“Chemtrails. I have told you a hundred times. It's a weather control thing not a poison the people thing.”

Oscar waves at person after person as they navigate past the makeshift storefronts. At one point he stops to chat with a heavy set bearded man standing next to an open space where an engine block is being dropped, over and over again, into a pile of sand.

“Hey Belcher.”

“Hey Oscar. You look unusually sober. Who are your friends?”

The man called Belcher is clearly eyeing Paige. She doesn’t look at all like she belongs here.

“David and Betty. Old friends. Don't you owe me some money for that gig in July?”

Belcher reaches out and grabs a four inch stack of flexible magnets wrapped in plastic. Each is about twice the size of a quarter.

“Have some magnets,” says Belcher, clearly unwilling to part with any cash.

“You're paying in magnets these days?” Even for Oscar this is too much. He grabs a second box and begins walking away.

“Hey, those are forty bucks each,” says Belcher.

“You still owe me two grand. Consider this interest. When I come to your shop next week you should have cash!” Oscar says as he walks away.

As they continue to walk, Paige catches up to Oscar.

“What are those?”

“Super magnets. Very handy. Two can lift four hundred pounds.”

They pass a stack of long thick laser pointers the size

of flashlights. *7 Watts* is written on the side of the blue cardboard box the pointers are in. There's also some kind of a warning label. Oscar picks up three, tosses one each to Paige and Richard, and then waves at the table owner who waves back.

"I just love the stuff at this show."

Paige has slipped her pointer out of the box. She presses the button required to turn it on and Oscar pushes her hand down so the light hits the ground. It leaves a scorch mark on the floor.

"Don't. They burn," he says.

Paige drops the empty box in a trash can and puts her pointer in a pocket.

Finally, in a far corner of the lobby, under a second set of escalators leading up to the second floor of the convention center, they find Janet.

She is in her late thirties with thin dishwater blond hair, a slim body, and a sharp, fierce face.

Oscar stops some distance away and turns to Richard.

"That's Janet. She and Eddie had a thing until early this year. They dated about a decade. If anyone knows what he was up to, I think maybe it is her."

Richard takes the lead as they approach. Janet is talking to a fifteen year old boy who is all of six feet tall and all of a hundred and forty pounds. He looks like he could be blown away by a brisk wind.

"I don't think solar flares have anything to do with it Sean."

"I sent you the specs and the drawings. You saw the design. It's perfect."

"We aren't talking about the design. We are talking about this phone."

"You wanted botchik voice encryption."

"I wanted a phone that could make a secure call. This one is so secure it can't call anyone."

"It works. I just used it yesterday."

"Well get it working again and bring it back. I'll be here all day."

The boy goes off muttering.

Janet turns to look at Oscar and her eyes widen in surprise and something that looks very much like hope.

"I was wondering if I would see you here. Have you seen Eddie? I have been so worried. He's not returning my calls."

"I'm so sorry, Janet," says Oscar.

Richard walks around the table and extends his

hand. “Hello. I’m so sorry we are meeting under these circumstances. I'm Richard. Eddie was my brother.”

Janet's eyes leap to his. “Was your brother?”

No one responds.

Janet looks for a moment as if she might cry, then she draws a deep breath, straightens up, and starts moving things around her shop. She sweeps a bunch of her phones into a box, pours out some cheap Wi-Fi hotspot devices, and then she drops into her chair again, arms crossed, She is suddenly shaking and fighting very hard not to weep.

“He was so stupid! He just wouldn't listen. I warned him a thousand times,” she manages to say.

“Was someone threatening him?” Richard asks.

Janet looks at Richard, eyes narrowing. “What makes you think I would say anything to you?” she hisses. “Never sent a letter or made a phone call. Not once in ten years. Not even an email.”

“We fought because I warned him that what he was doing was dangerous,” says Richard. “Just like you did.”

“You said his work would kill him. Maybe it did. There's no telling who he had to work for because he needed money and he needed help. You were his brother and you could have given everything he needed."

"Except I lost my father to that machine and I didn't want to lose my brother to it as well," Richard speaks the words and wonders yet again if he made a mistake. Eddie is dead and some business related to his work did kill him, but he was clearly on to something. Maybe he should have supported his brother's vision. But time and again it had always come down to the risks Eddie was willing to take that Richard found entirely unacceptable.

"If you had helped him then things would have been different," says Janet, her tone a bit less certain.

"Yes. By now we would both be dead," replies Richard, wondering if that is actually true. In hindsight he wishes he had moved heaven and earth to protect his brother.

Janet stands up again, moves to her cash box, pulls out the cash and starts to count it.
"Fine. You told me he's gone. You can go."

"I need to know what he was working on," says Richard.

Janet turns to look at him. "Why? What does it matter now?"

"Because the people that killed him are after us and we need something to bargain with."

Janet studies him for a long moment as if she can't

make out what kind of alien life form he might be. “So you're just going to hand over what Eddie died to protect?”

Richard looks at Oscar and Paige, then back at Janet. “Would it be better if we all died?”

Janet shakes her head. “I'm sorry. I can't help you. I don't know what he was working on. He never told me. I can probably tell you who killed him, but you won't like it.”

Richard's wonders if this can possibly be true. Armed with this information perhaps he can set up some kind of negotiation. This is information he certainly needs to know.

“Last year some men from up north made Eddie an offer he couldn't refuse.”

“What are you talking about?”

“A huge signing bonus, millions a year, his own research lab, a hand-picked team in return for all his work.”

“Who made the offer?”

“Some company. Arcanet, or ParNak. I don't remember. Doesn't matter really. The Global Elite. The G-Men. Many names for one face. The folks who think they own the world we live on.”

Richard studies her, recognizes her for the kook she

must be. Of course Eddie would fall in love with someone who shared his crazy theories.

“Do not pretend you do not know who I'm talking about, Richard. I know what you do. The kind of investments you make. Eddie was proud of you. Proud of your work even if he had a better way. Well the folks who write your paycheck, they killed your brother.”

“You don't know anything about the people I work for,” replies Richard. He tries to keep his tone level, but he knows his scorn is audible.

“How many people on this planet make the kind of money you spend? You work for a private consortium of investors. Maybe a thousandth of a percent on this planet make that much money. Well those folks who wanted to hire Eddie, they were military contractors, very well funded. Same class, same ivy league schools, same country clubs as the overlords you serve.”

“You're insane.” Richard hasn't heard the old saw that all the richest people in the world all know each other for so long he is at a loss for something to say.

“So. Get your answers somewhere else if you are so smart. Oscar knows your brother kept his work online. In the cloud they call it these days. Eddie could get it from everywhere, from anywhere. He put it in multiple places so it absolutely could not be lost, could not be destroyed. It was protected so it could not be stolen. You're such a genius. You find it." Janet turns to look at Oscar. "I never need to see you or these people ever again."

Richard studies Janet for a long moment. "You loved Eddie very much and I'm sure he loved you. I'm very sorry he and I put you at risk. It was unfair in every way to you."

Richard moves away from the table and Paige follows, rushing to take his hand.

Oscar moves closer to Janet. "It's not his fault Eddie is dead, Janet. That was Eddie's doing. Richard moved the world to save him."

"I don't blame him," Janet closes her eyes and the tears start. "But Eddie loved him so much. He used to talk about him all the time."

"If you loved Eddie you'll want to protect Richard," says Oscar. "He doesn't know what he's up against."

Janet sits down, wipes tears away with the back of her hand.

She reaches down, picks up a fully charged cell phone and tosses it to Oscar.

"It's untraceable, scrambled. If you can think of anyone to call, call them. Or dial nine zeroes you'll get to me. I won't be much help, but you never know. I wish I could have helped Eddie. I'd give anything to have him back."

Slowly she stands, reaches into a box, pulls out three exhibitor passes to the convention. These will get you in to see Duane. If anyone has answers he does."

"Thanks Janet."

Oscar gives her a bear hug and then leaves her standing alone at her table.

Oscar joins Richard and Paige near the entrance to the exhibition hall. Without a word he hands them the exhibitor passes. Together they walk past the convention hall guards.

Oscar, Richard and Paige walk through the exhibition hall which is filled with people demonstrating science toys and tools, cool high tech gadgets, and selling books to an audience of geeks and science fiction fans. Together they enter the *UFO Fact or Fiction* seminar to join several hundred people already in the theater who are listening to the end of the show.

Duane, a heavy set fifty-something dressed in a Hawaiian shirt and khaki shorts, is on stage addressing an audience member.

Oscar leans over to speak to Richard. "At last year's conference, Duane told me he was working with Eddie. I don't know for how long. But I figured you could ask him some questions."

"I don't know how you can say Area 51 isn't proof of

alien life," protests the thirty year old woman in the tie-dyed shirt.

"51 was a weapons lab. That's all," replies Duane dismissively.

"It was a crash site!" she says sharply.

"A plasma explosion. The government lost control of an experiment," Richard replies.

"What about the alien bodies?"

"Manufactured props. Don't be so gullible." Duane is clearly not in the mood to suffer fools gladly, and he is already looking for a way off stage as the announcer says, "Let's all have a round of applause for our great speaker!"

The crowd begins to clap and several people rise to give Duane a standing ovation.

Ignoring them, Duane hefts a heavy black doctor's bag and begins making his way toward the edge of the stage. As he exits stage left, three new speakers enter stage right. One carries a cardboard alien.

The announcer comes back on to say, "Everyone? Listen up! Please clear the room if you do not have tickets to the International SETI panel. We'll be starting in just four minutes."

Paige, Oscar, and Richard move quickly through the crowd, managing to meet Duane just as he steps off the last step and turns toward the conference room's rear exit. He has some kind of injury involving both ankles, so he lumbers a bit. Duane sees Oscar approaching, but pretends not to, and he picks up speed despite his awkward gait, apparently determined to outmaneuver a much more able man.

As he steps out into the service corridor behind the stage, Oscar calls out.

"Hey, Duane! Do you have a minute?"

Duane continues walking fast but Oscar catches up to him.

Unable to ignore him any longer, Duane says, "Hey Oscar. Are you still souping up the carnival rides?"

"I should be so lucky. I am seasonally unemployed," Oscar replies amiably.

"If you're off the sauce, send me your resume."

By this time Richard and Paige are walking beside Oscar and Duane in the otherwise empty corridor. Duane looks grimmer by the minute. As he continues walking, he says, "Who are your little pals?"

Richard takes a few quick steps to move to the other side of the waddling man.

"Do you have a minute to talk? Somewhere private?"

"Who's asking?" Duane demands, directing the question at Oscar.

“Eddie's brother.”

Duane turns to look Richard up and down.

“Eddie's dead and I don't want you within a hundred miles of me.”

“Give me two minutes,” says Richard. “You never have to see me again.”

“I've got nothing to tell you. I stopped working with that crazy loon six months ago. Everything he did blew up,” replies Duane coldly.

Richard puts a hand on Duane's shoulder to stop him. Duane knocks it off.

“We both know Eddie so we both know that's not true,” Richard says firmly.

“Stay away from me,”

Duane turns and starts walking toward one of the other conference rooms, clearly unwilling to be alone with the three of them any more.

Richard stops walking and calls out, “If we get picked up I'll give them your name.”

Duane stops, turns around, looks at Oscar, Paige then Richard. He glances up at a security camera.

“What the hell do you want? I'd rather spend two

minutes with Plutonium than with you. You have exactly sixty seconds to say whatever you want to say, and then we are done."

"My brother was working on something. I think you know what it was. Now he's dead and someone thinks I have it. If I did have it, I could cut some kind of deal."

"So you want to hand over what Eddie died for," says Duane.

Richard gestures at Paige. "My wife didn't sign up to save the world with free energy. Neither did I. We were drafted and suddenly we're on the front lines of a war for a technology we neither understand nor believe in."

"Maybe it's time you started believing, Richard. Eddie was pretty smart and the guys who killed him think he has something."

"It's a potent dream. We see lightning in the sky and wonder why can't we draw it down. I've no doubt Eddie believed. Or that he could convince others to believe. But if his technology worked why not just make it freely available? Why all the cloak and dagger?"

Duane cocks his head to one side, stares at Richard for a long moment. "That is exactly what Eddie said."

"What?" Richard is shocked.

Duane takes in that Richard has no idea what he's talking about, and suddenly he's back to his original tack.

"Look, I haven't worked with Eddie for months. Some goons came by and said he was starting up some kind of new lab for the military. They wanted me on board. I said no, and it took me a couple of months to convince them I was technically inept and a gibbering idiot before they left me alone. When I heard Eddie was dead I hit the road. New phone, new card, living on cash. I wouldn't even let them put me on the program here because I didn't want that out on the net. I've been a surprise guest all day."

"What was Eddie working on?" Richard asks.

"What he was always worked on of course. Harvester technology. And I think you are out of luck. If Eddie hid something from you, you'll never find it. He was brilliant."

"I'm told he kept everything online."

"It's a huge internet. Last I heard he could put something on the net on one server and it would be transferred overnight to others, sometimes a million packets at a time. Pieces of it would be on this university computer, on that corporate computer, on an overseas bank server. He scattered and backed up his body of work across the internet, entirely encrypted, moving it hour after hour, day after day."

"Then how did Eddie find it?"

"He knew what to look for and where to look, of course." Then, as if unable to stop himself, Duane continues. "You know, I hope you don't sell your brother out. He was a good guy and he died for something that mattered."

"Really? What?" Richard feels like he is finally talking to someone who knows what is actually going on.

Duane looks at each of them one by one. When he speaks again, it is directly to Richard. "It's a hungry world, and a thirsty world, and a little power in a lot of hands would make a huge difference. That's the last thing Eddie told me."

Duane looks at the cameras continuously watching the hall, shrugs, and says "Well, that's all I have for you. Goodbye. I hope I never see any of you again." Then he is back to waddling his way down and out of the hall.

* * *

Wilde is looking out his window and down at a

shop floor where a dozen large vaguely ant-shaped creatures tower over the men walking below them. From here it's clear to see this is a Harvester farm based on Eddie's design.

Wilde has his cell phone pressed to his ear. "Why did it take you so long to find them?"

Colonel White is on his cell phone. He's standing where Janet's booth used to be. It's been cleaned out. Just empty boxes and tape remain.

"The power was out everywhere which meant there was only spotty cell service. We couldn't track his phone or the girl's until they hit a hot zone. They only hit this network two hours ago and we've already tracked them here."

"So pick them up," says Wilde as if it is the easiest thing on earth to do.

"We have alerted convention security and I'm doing a sweep now. All the entrances are guarded and I have checkpoints."

A beep interrupts them.

"I don't care how the sausage is made. I just need them back here immediately. Stop screwing around Colonel," says Wilde, and then he disconnects to answer the incoming call.

"Yes?"

“Doctor? General Tyson has indicated he and General Birch will be arriving tomorrow at two.”

* * *

Oscar leads Richard and Paige down a set of escalators past a sign that says INTERNET LOUNGE.

Down in the basement there are ten long tables, each supporting a dozen workstations and people who have plugged in their own laptops. Behind the tables are gaming kiosks that reach from floor to ceiling and sport chairs for gamers to sit in as they play. Behind that is a curtained area for exhibitors.

The room is filled to overflowing and people are standing, sitting, and talking everywhere.

Richard takes a seat at a workstation at a table as far as possible from the front door.

“I don't know where to begin to look for whatever Eddie was hiding. Do you know anything at all Oscar?”

“Eddie used to log me in when we had to work. He would search for something online, then click on it, and play some kind of video game. Then I would have access for a little while. It was all very secure.”

“Why didn't you mention all this sooner?”

"I didn't think it mattered. Eddie did lots of strange things."

Richard studies the search engine before him. "He had to be looking for something unique."

Richard begins to type. A search for Eddie Maxwell yields page titles like E*ddie Maxwell Free Energy Lecture at Radicon, Eddie Maxwell Lectures on Energy Independence in the New Millenia, Eddie Maxwell, Energy for Everyman.*

Richard clicks on the links and sees pictures of Eddie lecturing. His brother looks passionate, driven, happy.

"I guess it's too much to hope that it would be called something like Eddie Maxwell Secret Data," says Paige.

"You never know. We used to tell Eddie he should go completely underground. Change his name, have surgery to alter his appearance. But he said it was much easier to hide in plain sight," replies Oscar.

"Who was he hiding from? Our government? Other governments? Criminals?" she asks.

"Is there a difference?"

Richard looks up at Oscar as if he is insane.

"Sorry," the old radical says apologetically.

Richard looks back at the screen, continues to click through links, glances at pictures. "It will be something completely obvious that I'll kick myself for not knowing right away. Eddie's work is always like that."

Richard reaches into his pocket, pulls out the scorpion cube, sets it on the table. "Wake up."

In an instant the creature has unfolded itself.

"Will you look at that!" says Oscar, entirely delighted.

"Has it occurred to you that your brother is fixated on insects?" Paige asks. "Maybe that's something to look into."

Richard speaks to the scorpion. "Password," he tries.

Nothing happens.

"Can it talk?" Paige asks. "It's never done that, has it?"

Richard looks at Oscar then back at the bug. "Talk!"

Nothing happens.

"This thing has to be the key somehow," says Richard.

"Does it have an adapter? Can you plug it into the computer?" asks Oscar.

Richard picks the device up, turns it over. He studies

it closely as it's legs wriggle. Then puts it down. "I knows It's staring me right in the face. Jesus Eddie, what are you trying to say?"

From outside the curtained enclosure, there's a sudden collective silence punctuated only by video games that continue to kill as their operators stop moving.

Richard looks over his monitor toward the door. He sees Colonel White and a cadre of ten men in black have entered the room. Armed with semi-automatics, they wave people away from the door.

Richard drops his head back down, snatches up the scorpion, and drops to the floor. Oscar and Paige, seeing the move instinctively drop as well.

Together they hear Colonel White say, "This is a homeland security operation. We are seeking fugitives."

Richard looks at the scorpion which is trying to crawl out of his hand. "Sleep!" he orders.
The scorpion folds up and Richard hands it to Oscar.

Who drops it, shaking his hand as if it has been stung. His surprise is evident.

"It shocked me!" he says.

"It does that. Isn't it annoying?" says Paige.

Colonel White and his men are walking through the

room, looking at every face.

Under the table Richard stuffs the scorpion cube into his pocket. Then he says, “You two have to get out of here.”

“How?” Oscar asks curiously.

“What about you?” asks Paige.

“They only want me. They'll let you walk out.”

“I don't think so,” says Oscar.

“No!” whispers Paige, clearly shocked that he is asking her to abandon him.

Colonel White, having been through the room without finding Richard, studies one of the tables. He uses his foot to stir the curtain.

“Whatever they want, they killed Eddie for! I don't want them to have it. I don't want them to have you either.”

Richard looks at Oscar. “I'm going to create a distraction. You know the layout of this place. Get her out of here.”

“I said No!” Paige’s voice is a little louder and both men flinch.

“Paige, once they have you, the negotiation's over. They win. You are the ball game for me. I don’t care about anything or anyone else as much as I care about you."

Oscar pulls the black cell phone out of his pocket. He dials a number. "We need help getting out of Fort Knox," he whispers.

"What are you doing?" Richard demands.

"Hopefully getting us all out of this," replies Oscar. Then he speaks into the phone, "Ok. Exhibitor loading dock in five."

Oscar terminates the call and hands it to Richard. "Dial nine nines to find me," he says. Then he looks at Paige. "We should go."

Paige leans over to take Richard's hand. She opens her mouth to speak.

Richard holds up his hand for silence. There's a black boot just outside their curtain.

Richard pulls the laser Oscar gave him earlier out of his pocket. He moves the table curtain aside and points it outside. A hot white laser light appears on a curtain just past one of the Men in Black. In a few seconds, the curtain catches fire as well. Richard redirects the laser light to another curtain close to the front door of the room. It catches fire. Suddenly people all over the room are shrieking.

"Remain where you are!" Colonel White is now issuing orders to a room filled with people who are more afraid of burning to death than being shot.

Oscar tugs at Paige's arm and together they start crawling under the tables toward the exit. Richard crawls the opposite direction. The sprinklers come on and people start shrieking. A siren blares.

Richard reaches a wall and starts moving along it. He reaches the midpoint, moves some boxes and finds a power outlet, he aims the laser inside. The overhead lights go off, and the large room is suddenly lit only by floor-mounted emergency lights.

Colonel White, standing in the middle of the room, watches panicking people shoving one another out the double doors and emergency exits. Looking around the room, he starts overturning tables without regard to what might fall on the floor. After a second's confusion his men follow suit.

A few minutes later, soaked to the skin, Richard walks outside the convention center. The black phone is pressed to his ear.

"Oscar?"

"Hilton parking lot, across the street. I'll find you," replies Janet.

Richard looks around, sees the Hilton sign and begins walking toward it.

Janet drives along the Las Vegas strip, glancing into her mirrors frequently.

“You folks are way more trouble than you are worth,” she says.

“Not me, them,” says Oscar, gesturing to the couple in the back seat.

“Where are you taking us?” Richard asks.

“Right now I'm driving randomly through cell zones. Does anyone in this car have a cell phone?”

Janet and Richard dig in sodden pockets and both hold up their smartphones.

“Rookies,” says Oscar wryly. “Sorry I didn't ask hours ago.”

“Please throw them outside,” she says.

Reluctantly Paige and Richard both comply.

“For the record, they can track you with those. You know that right? Also, just because you aren't talking doesn't mean they aren't listening.”

Janet shakes her head, clearly worried about what might come next. “Let's hope they follow your electronic footprints when your phones get stolen and that they don’t know anything at all about me.”

She looks up into her mirror. “So, got a plan, Maxwell?”

“Not really,” he admits.

Janet signs and heads toward the highway.

* * *

Richard and Paige are sitting side by side on a broken down couch that rests on a dilapidated porch overlooking a swath of lake and weeds. Oscar leans against a peeling rail a few feet away. He's playing with a lighter. He fills his hand with puffs of gas, then sets it alight.

“He's going to burn himself,” says Paige.

“The flame is too cool and it's not in his hand long enough,” says Richard reassuringly. “When Eddie and I were kids, Dad's friends would show us that kind of thing all the time. Everyone was Mr. Science. Eddie loved it. I got bored.”

“Were you and Eddie really that much different?” Paige asked.

“When you're trapped with your brother day after day, year after year, It's always a struggle for identity. Someone has to be the good one, someone the bad one, someone the smart one, someone the artistic one. Eddie was the eager, interested, open kid. I was the bored jerk.” Richard shakes his head, sits forward. He reaches in his pocket and pulls out the cube.

"Wake up." The box becomes the scorpion.

"This is elegant. It's brilliant. It's just Eddie all over. And that makes it a mystery to me. What was he trying to say?"

"What's that?" Janet asks.

Richard holds out his hand to show the bug to her. He rolls his hand from palm up to palm down and the scorpion adjusts its position to stay on top.

"Eddie sent it to me."

Janet rises, comes to look at it. She reaches out to touch it. Paige waves her off.

"Don't. It shocks people."

Oscar comes over to look at it too.

"Looks like the repair drones in the old lab. They were bigger, slower."

Janet looks at Richard.

"I didn't know you were talking to him before he died."

Richard shakes his head. Paige responds for him.

"It came in the mail."

Janet looks at Richard, then rises.

"Eddie was a good guy," Richard says "Just completely impractical. He wanted a better world and he wanted it now. He took risk after risk. I could never understand that. I hate the idea that someone might get hurt on one of my projects. Big or small, anywhere in the world. Safety first."

"Some risks are worth taking," says Janet.

"A project like the Harvester needs serious investment. The kind only governments can make It's not a bunch of guys building a monster in a tin can in the middle of the desert."

"Eddie didn't make monsters. He made miracles," Janet replies. It's clear that she thinks she is stating the obvious.

Richard studies the rhythmic movement of the scorpion as he passes it from one hand to the other. "I suppose he did."

Janet stands up.

"I'm exhausted. It's been a long time since I had guests, but I believe I can make you all comfortable for the night."

She walks into the house leaving the door open behind her. Oscar, Richard, and Paige rise after a moment and follow her in.

Richard and Paige are in bed. She has her eyes closed and he is staring at the ceiling. They are newly washed and their hair is wet.

"You have to sleep, Richard."

"I can't believe I put you in this position." The thought that he might, after all is said and done, actually have involved Paige in another Maxwell family disaster is deeply troubling to him. He would do anything, sacrifice anything, to have that not be the case.

Paige turns over, kisses his shoulder. Eyes still closed, she speaks. "There's no place I'd rather be than here. I've spent my life fighting for lost causes. Built my career on them. Eddie's dream seems like something worth fighting for."

Richard shakes his head. "Honey, I don't know what's going to happen. They can arrest us, hold us indefinitely. We're terrorists."

She sits up and props her head on one hand.

"No we aren't. Just because someone sticks a label on you doesn't make it so. Eddie wasn't making a bomb. You don't want to hurt anyone. You have something they want. That's all. Something they'll do anything to get. But you'll find a way out. Watch and see."

Richard pulls her head down so it rests against his shoulder and she closes her eyes again. He kisses her and she snuggles up against him.

Richard's eyes remain fixed on the ceiling. Paige's faith in him somehow makes everything worse.

* * *

It is morning. No one else is awake for a long time. Richard, fully dressed in freshly laundered clothes, waits in the kitchen. Janet comes in and pours herself some of the coffee he's brewed.

“Can you drive me into town? I need to get online.”

“Why?”

“There's something I want to try.”

Janet looks away, nods, rises.

“Let's go,” she says.

As Janet and Richard pull into the parking lot of an office building, Richard looks around at all the empty spaces.

“This is a billing annex for the local phone company. Landlines only. No one is here on a Sunday morning, but it’s got a T3 connection to the internet and I have some software that will give you some anonymity.”

“That's handy. You seem to have a lot of ways to fly under the radar,” he says.

“Eddie and I met a decade ago when he was shopping for broadband access that couldn't be tracked,” she replies.

"And that's something you could offer him?"

"Did you ever notice that governments are all about protecting their secrets and stealing yours?"

Janet pulls into a parking space and Richard gets out.

Janet leads Richard to a desk in a cubicle on the third floor of the building. Outside the window her car can be seen in the parking lot. She sits down at a workstation, types a few characters, clicks on something. "Now any page you hit will think you are coming in from Bern Switzerland. I have a tunnel into a server there."

"Great."

Janet stands up and lets Richard take her chair.

Richard removes the cube from his pocket and says, "Wake up."

The scorpion unfolds. Richard turns to look at Janet. She stares at the screen expectantly.
Richard stares at it too, glances at the scorpion, and begins typing.

His first connection is to a search engine. He types in a string of numbers and a series of pages come up. He clicks on the first three or four of the listed pages in succession, but doesn't find what he's looking for.

He sits back, studies the scorpion. After a time the

colors on the triangles swim. His brain is struggling to turn colors into letters which it finds a most unnatural thing.

He leans forward and tries a search for T E A R E S. Nothing comes up. He tries T E Q R E S. Nothing again. Then he tries S E R Q E T.

This search brings up new pages that reference the Egyptian goddess of Scorpions. Heart pounding, Richard clicks the image search button. On the first page of a long list of images he finds a photo of the scorpion that sits before him.

Richard clicks the image and he is taken to a page where a picture of Eddie's pretty little scorpion fills the screen.

Janet looks at it, then at Richard.

Richard clicks on the scorpion and a series of multicolored squares start to fill the screen. Janet suddenly reaches under the desk to turn the computer off.

“What are you doing?”

Janet gestures at something outside the building. A helicopter is flying low and fast toward them and black cars are pulling into the parking lot.

There's the sound of glass breaking somewhere in the building. Richard looks at the scorpion on the desk. "Sleep," he says and the scorpion folds up.

Richard stuffs it in his pocket and he follows Janet through acres of cubicles toward a bank of elevators. Before they reach them, the doors slide open and four men in black combat uniforms come on to the floor. Richard and Janet both duck down.

Crouching, Janet leads Richard into a computer room. She pulls up part of the floor in one corner to reveal a long drop to the floor below. She slips through the gap and Richard follows. He hangs from the ceiling grid just long enough to slide the floor plate above them back into place.

“In the basement there's a passthrough to the next building,” says Janet as she walks Richard across the hall to the staircase that leads down. She starts to enter and he stops her.

“You've done enough,” he says.

“What are you talking about?”

“They don't want you. They want me. If Eddie had wanted you involved, he'd have sent you the message. He didn't. He sent it to me.”

Janet stares at him.

“He wanted you safe. So it's time for you to go underground now. Thank you for all your help. Eddie was very lucky to have you and I wish I’d had the opportunity to know you better.“

Richard enters the stairway alone and the door closes behind him.

The basement is filled with thick conduits and racks of wires and equipment lockers. The concrete floor echoes as Richard walks. As he enters the sloping underground passageway to the unnamed neighboring building, Richard hears something.

He turns to find Colonel White following him down the corridor. The two men In black with the Colonel are armed, and White carries a military issue nightstick.

Richard stops walking, raises his hands over his head. “Fine. I give up. You got me.”

Colonel White continues to walk toward him. When they meet, Colonel White bashes Richard across the face with the stick.

As Richard drops, he says. “I lost nine men to your monster.”

CHAPTER 6

Richard, lying on a narrow couch in the corporate jet, wakes up. His hand comes to the side of his head which is badly bruised. He starts to sit up then falls back again. His eyes close.

Duane, Paige and Oscar, strapped into seats nearby, all have their wrists bound with plastic ties. Duane's black bag rests between his feet.

"Well, at least he's not dead," says Duane.

"Richard? Are you Okay? Where did you go? Why didn't you take me with you?" Paige leans forward as far as she can without getting up. One of White's men sits behind the captives armed with a club and she looks over her shoulder at the man when he pulls her back into her seat.

"He might have a concussion!"

"Sit down," orders Colonel White.

Richard opens his eyes, struggles into a seated position, and looks at Paige. “I'm fine.”

Richard looks anything but well as he moves into one of the standard airplane seats. He turns to look out the window at a darkening sky.

* * *

Later Oscar, Paige, and Duane are all looking out the window. Richard is sleeping with his head against the glass.

“We are very far north,” says Oscar.

“Arctic circle. About 20 degrees latitude, judging by the time of day and the stars.” says Duane.

“Alaska? Canada?” Paige asks.

“Alaska. We're not being kidnapped by Canucks,” says Duane.

“Stop talking,” orders Colonel White.

Richard opens his eyes at the sound of Colonel White's voice. He turns his head to look out the window. Below him is a marshy arctic waste surrounding a military base featuring two dozen hangers and what looks like a large concrete and steel office building.

The pilot comes on the radio. “We're making our final approach. Please take your seats.”

“Please?” notes Duane. “I've never been abducted so politely.”

The plane starts to descend.

“Now pay attention boys and girls, because the real fun is about to begin,” says Richard without opening his eyes.

Richard, escorted by Colonel White and two base MPs walks across the tarmac to an elevator. Paige, Duane and Oscar follow several hundred feet behind, shepherded by a single guard in front and another one behind. Both are armed. Duane carries his bag awkwardly before him and his mangled legs are clearly giving him trouble.

Once the elevator doors close, Richard watches Colonel White press the button for the top floor of the facility.

“I'm meeting the big boss I guess,” he says.

Colonel White and the two guards ignore him.

“Good. Always go straight to the top. That's my motto.”

Minutes later, Duane shifts uneasily from foot to foot as they wait for the elevator Richard disappeared into not so long ago.

"Are you okay?" Oscar asks.

"Cold makes my bones hurt," Duane replies.

"They don't have a treatment for that?"

Duane turns to look at him. "Yes. They do. Lots of magnesium. I have to carry it with me."

"Really? I'm glad you've got something that helps." replies Oscar complacently.

The doors open, and Duane picks up his bag and holds it bottom out as he steps inside. He turns as Oscar and Paige enter. Oscar crowds Paige into the elevator's back wall, and before the guards can enter there is a huge explosion of white fire from the base of Duane's bag.

The soldiers fall back, their clothes on fire. The doors close on them as they fight the flames.

Duane presses all the buttons on the elevator. It chooses to go down first.

Duane drops his bag and jerks it open as the elevator doors open on the first floor below the tarmac. Duane, Oscar, and Page ignore the long halls outside the parted doors as Duane searches his bag. He finds a heavy duty swiss army knife. In a second a blade is open. He turns to Oscar who holds out his hands. Duane cuts the binders. Oscar returns the favor then cuts Paige free. By this time the doors have closed.

Duane pulls a bunch of objects out of the bag and shoves them in his pockets. When the elevator opens on the second floor below the tarmac he steps out, leaving the bag behind. Oscar and Paige follow suit.

As the doors close, Oscar slaps four of the disk shaped magnets he got from the expo on the edges of the door. The next time the elevator arrives on this floor, the doors won't open because the magnets will effectively glue them shut with a thousand pounds of magnetic force.

Now alone on the second floor under ground, Oscar, Duane, and Paige look around. They are in a concrete hall way that extends in four directions. They look down the hall straight ahead and see a row of doors. At the end of the hall there are double doors large enough to drive a truck through. Oscar strides to the nearest door along the hall and tries to open it. It's locked. Paige, perceiving his objective, runs to the next door on the opposite side of the hall. She has no luck there either. Oscar tries a third door. It opens on a locker room.

* * *

Richard, hands now unbound, sits in a leather chair in Wilde's elegant office. The curtains are drawn to hide the lab floor. The curtains over the window that overlook the airfield and base are uncovered. Richard rises to look out at the tarmac. He sees a fire burning and men rushing to extinguish it with white foam.

Colonel White, arms crossed, watches him from a position near the door. The MPs stand at attention nearby.

Richard speaks without looking at Colonel White. "You killed my brother."

"He killed himself. He was driving the wrong way on the highway."

"I meant in the helicopter. You wanted to bring him here." Richard turns to look at him.

White says nothing.

Richard looks out at the base again, watches a military fire truck driving up to put out the flames.

The door behind him opens and closes. Richard turns around to face Wilde and for a moment, he feels overwhelming relief. Then that emotion fades to something between fury and despair.

"Relax Richard. You're among friends."

Richard looks pointedly at Colonel White, then back at Wilde. "Really?"

“You can't call us strangers Richard. The Yang Tse, Angel Falls, the Denver Dam, the new Brazilian project. We've been working together for decades.”

“Strange. I feel I hardly know you.”

Wilde walks to his desk, pulls open the curtains, invites Richard to look down on the factory floor.

“Look at them. Aren't they beautiful? Based on designs created by your father and brother.”

Richard stares down at the monsters which look like cleaner versions of the thing that almost killed him forty-eight hours ago. “Have you turned them on? It goes badly. One was quite a handful I thought. Don't know what you'll do with the dozens you have down there.”

“We can produce at 1% over unity. For every megawatt we put in, we get 1.1 megawatt out. Pure, clean, raw power.“

Richard returns to his chair, regards Wilde with the machines hulking behind him.

“Great. So, why am I here.”

“Because we both know your brother had something better. I funded his work for years, provided him with logistical and technical support through a variety of third parties. When his work reached a critical stage and I offered him a more direct relationship along with a sizable advance. He disappeared taking what I had paid for with him."

"How does this concern me? You must know how I felt about Eddie's work."

"We think, which is to say, I know, he gave you what I paid for."

"What on earth makes you think that? We never spoke. Not once in more than a decade. No contact at all."

"He sent you a package."

"With a map to the facility in Arizona which had one of those monsters in it. He was a mad man."

"What else did you find there?"

"Dr. Wilde, my brother was insane. Like my father. You understand that, right? What they wanted to invent, what they kept trying to create, was a perpetual motion machine. Start it up and it will run forever. That's not how the world works. We know that. You may have something you think works, but I don't believe it."

"What was in his lab?"

"Nothing! Wire, rusty tools, the toys of a lunatic. If you got that thing working it's more than Eddie ever did."

“He wasn't crazy Richard. He was brilliant. Misguided, tragically idealistic, but brilliant. We need, the world needs his next step. I can't believe he would let himself die without passing it on. You're the last person he tried to contact. I need to know what he said.”

Richard looks out the window at the machines.

“Now I'm wondering how much of my life was a lie. It's not a coincidence that my consortium of investors is chaired by a man who has built a career stealing my brother's work.“

“I worked with your Dad in his earliest days, followed him after he left the military. We were friends on different tracks. Me working within the system, him running from it. He died leaving two sons and I knew their worth. I found a way to help you and Eddie both. You had no interest in your father's work and Eddie did. I supported you each in doing the work you most wanted to do.”

The office intercom beeps. Wilde presses a button on his desk.

“Yes?”

The secretary says, “Your guests have arrived Doctor.”

“Thank you.”

Wilde turns to Richard.

"Like your father and your brother, you're a good man and an exceptional engineer. I need you to help me solve a problem. Your brother promised me something that I promised to someone else. He subsequently vanished."

"So you told the feds he was a terrorist?"

"Eddie threatened to release what I'd paid for to the rest of the world. In the wrong hands, that would be a bomb."

"What are you talking about?"

"Every terrorist in the world armed with infinite power? Every dictator? Every criminal? Eddie never understood the realities of what he was proposing."

Richard shakes his head and looks down at the army of monsters Wilde has built.

"Ah. Now I see. Unlimited power belongs only in the hands of the *right* people."

* * *

Oscar, dressed in what looks like white clean room scrubs, walks down the hall dragging two heavy garbage cans on wheels that are overstuffed with plastic bags. As he moves down the hall he tries each of the doors, just a janitor making his rounds.

Far behind him the elevator doors are being banged on.

"Well, I guess now they know what floor we got off on."

Oscar walks faster, now heading directly for the double doors at the end of the hall.

"What is this place?" asks one of the bags.

"Weapons lab of some kind. Not munitions," says the other.

"Security is very loose," says Oscar.

"Who is going to sneak in. And where can anyone run to? Only way in or out is by plane. Every plane that lands here is a military flight. Sooner or later they are going to catch us."

"Oscar steps through the double doors an instant before the elevator doors behind him are pried open.

Oscar stares up at the giant machines, which, from this angle look like a forest of three story white ants with spiky metal balls for heads. Each is grounded to the floor by thick black electrical cables.

"I thought one was more than enough."

Richard, hands in his pockets, stares out the window at the machines. Wilde stands at his side.

“No one knows better than I do how motivated you are to solve problems that will save lives.”

Richard turns to look at him.

“I need the technology I paid for. I know Eddie kept his data online, that it moves continuously, and that he intended you to find it.”

“He didn't tell me where to look.”

“Downstairs I have two Generals. I've promised them, as your brother once promised me, the moon. My career, my entire life, is on the line. So your life and the lives of your friends are on the line too. You didn't want anything to do with Eddie's work. I invested hundreds of millions of dollars in it.” Wilde steps back, gestures at his workstation. “You are going to give us both what we always wanted.”

Richard removes his hands from his pockets, walks toward the workstation, and sits down.

Wilde looks at Colonel White. “Shoot him if he tries to leave. He knows enough to be dangerous.”

Wilde leaves the room and Richard stares at the screen.

* * *

The lab is the length and width of two spongy football fields. The field of ants takes up most of the space. A forest of tall black boxes fill one corner and it is near these that Oscar Paige and Duane are standing.

"What's this spongy stuff on the floor?" Paige asks.

"Several feet of rubber. It's non-conductive. Think of the bugs as lightning collectors, or lightning generators if you prefer. They want the electricity to go into the wires rather than striking all around the room," says Duane.

"You wouldn't want anyone to get electrocuted," says Oscar.

"Are you sure? Maybe I would," replies Paige.

A siren begins to wail and instinctively they all look back toward the double doors. A red light is now spinning. Duane walks to the closest large black box. He runs his hands over it as he walks around it. Paige and Duane join him. Their hands also explore the rubber covered surface.

Standing in the black cushioned cave between two boxes Duane shakes his head.

"I think if they were willing to use all hands on base to find us, they would have us already. I think someone is trying to find us quietly, which means those sirens are because someone is starting a test."

"Are we safe?" Paige asks.

“Here? Of course not. You're an electrical field. Don't you think it might be a bit disrupting to stand in a forest of electrical generators hard at work? That's not good for people.”

Paige presses her hand against the closest monolith which looks like something out of 2001 a Space Odyssey.

“These won't protect us?”

“These are capacitors and batteries. This is where all the power goes.”

Oscar is studying the boxes. “If we break something, what happens? Do they stop the test?”

Duane looks at Oscar and then at the boxes. “He shakes his head as if he's doubting his sanity. It would stop the test, that's for sure. I suspect these are lithium, unless they are developing a new bulk energy storage technology as well.”

Duane walks through the forest of vertical slabs to the battery closest to the Harvester army. He pulls out his heavy duty pocket knife, and starts cutting into the insulation directly across from the bugs. As he pulls chunks of the soft black rubber away, it's clear that the insulation is more than a foot thick.

Oscar holds up his laser. “Shall we try fire?” He focuses the white light on the rubber and it melts the insulation as if were butter.

Duane looks at him with new respect. “Good help is so hard to find.”

Oscar smiles, steps to the side of the slab, and aims his laser so he can shave a large swathe of insulation off the front of the battery in one stroke.

Paige looks toward the door where the red light is still spinning. She turns and looks up at the Harvesters. They’ve begun shifting position as if looking for some invisible wind. Ropes of blue lightning are beginning to crawl from their pin-covered heads down their long legs to the cables in the ground.

“I still don't quite see how this works out well for us,” says Paige softly.

* * *

Richard scoots his chair closer to the computer and pulls the colored cube from his pocket. “Wake up,” he says softly and the cube unfolds. The Scorpion crawls up off the desk and on to Richard’s hand. Colonel White sees some part of the motion and comes to look over his shoulder.

“What's that?”

“A clue, maybe.”

While the Colonel looks at the scorpion, Richard

uses the computer keyboard to search for Serqet, the scorpion goddess who can both hurt and heal. This is the perfect name for the tiny mechanical creature before him. Eddie intended his masterpiece to both create and destroy. Everything is starting to make sense now.

Richard finds and clicks on a photo of Eddie's scorpion, then studies the brightly colored scorpion as it dances on the screen. He pauses for a moment to look out into the lab, sees wide bands of lightning crawling up and down the Harvesters in an orderly, laconical, entirely well-behaved way.

Richard clicks the scorpion dancing on screen and is given a page that is all one color. Mystified he clicks. The page changes to another color. Richard sighs, sits back, and starts clicking faster.

“What are you doing?”

“Learning,” replies Richard. Richard cycles through a series of 36 non-repeating colors. An alphabet and numbers.

After the third pass, the pattern changes. Intuitively he deciphers the sentence using the code he just learned. It says, *type 31363 to deploy designs worldwide* and *type 999999 to open a working archive*. Wondering what to do, where Paige, Duane, and Oscar are, and how they are all going to get out of here, Richard just stares at the screen.

* * *

Wilde, the Generals, their aides and a half dozen operators watch the machines run from the relative safety of a control room just off the lab floor. Another loud crack occurs as the operators follow Wilde's instructions to let the Harvesters produce more power. One of the Generals leans over to speak to Wilde. "What was that?"

"Electrostatic discharge. Perfectly normal."

"Another crack echoes, but Wilde speaks over it. As you can see, gentlemen, we are 1% over unity. The units are producing power. As we bring the system down you'll notice that all systems cleanly stop cycling."

"Continue the test. I want to see what we've been paying for," says General Birch. He's always reminded Wilde of a schoolyard bully, with his bald bullet head and stocky body, but never more so than today.

"General Birch, I must insist," says Wilde. "This is expensive equipment.

General Tyson, who is a tall, pale, corpse of a man says, "You've got one percent. We need two. We want undeniable proof it works, Doctor."

* * *

Paige is trying to push her way through the double doors. They appear to be locked, probably to ensure no one walks onto the lab floor during a test. The light over her head is flashing red, garishly illuminating Oscar and Duane as they come up behind her.

A very loud crack makes all three saboteurs look over their shoulders with concern. "A long arc of lightning reaches out from the closest ant to strike the newly exposed metal skin of a battery closest to it."

"Our plan has serious flaws," says Oscar.

"Why aren't they shutting this thing down?" Paige wonders out loud. "They must know something is wrong."

"Maybe they can't."

"We have to get this door open," says Duane, stepping back.

Just then the double doors part to reveal three of Colonel White's men in black along with a team of five firefighters dragging hoses behind them.

* * *

Wilde is pointing at one of the meters. "Two point five percent. We've more than doubled our output, General."

"Not by much. And look at your lab. Where there's that much smoke there's usually a fire," says General Birch with apparent satisfaction.

One of the Lab Assistants rises. "Doctor, we have a short circuit on battery three."

"That's not unexpected. Just shut the system down," says Wilde. Nothing matters beyond getting the devices to stop producing power before it overloads.

The technicians in the control room move to obey. It's clear, from their behavior, that a short circuit is not at all to be expected. In fact it is a very bad thing.

"This looks like a circus to me, Doctor, and you appear to be a clown." General Tyson is seeing firefighters enter the lab floor dragging their hoses filled with white foam.

"General, I don't think you understand what you're seeing."

"I certainly do. Fraud, misappropriation of government funds, outright theft, gross incompetence."

"I assure you that is not correct. You're looking at decades of research, entirely new technologies."

"One day you can try to explain it to a judge."

"Doctor, batteries three through six are fusing. The input is being rerouted to the other units but they are heating up." The operator at the end of the first row looks to be on the edge of panic as she reviews this information. She's a new hire and Wilde makes a note to fire her as soon as the Generals leave.

"Doctor Wilde, I've cycled the system but somehow power output is increasing," says the lab floor manager. "The safety systems are failing."

"How can this thing melt down?" General Tyson asks. "Critical failure is supposed to lead to automatic shut down. Isn't that right Doctor?"

They all look into the room. The mechanical ants are now coated with a thick sheen of blue plasma. Long streaks of lightning are repeatedly striking the batteries. The sea of foam being shot at the machines and the batteries is having no effect.

The new hire at the end of the first row pipes up again. "Now batteries three through eleven are fused, Dr. Wilde. Capacitors are shorting."

* * *

Richard is standing, looking down at the floor of overloading harvesters. Colonel White and his men are watching the show as well. No one in the room is particularly surprised to see that things have gone wrong.

They are somewhat surprised when Wilde strides into the room. Behind him, Paige, Duane, and Oscar are being shoved into the room by men in black.

“Where's my data!” demands Dr. Wilde, striding toward Richard as if he intends physical violence.

The computer that rests on Wilde’s desk is flashing the names of university websites worldwide. One right after another in a sequence so rapid the letters blur. Colors scroll by in bands at the bottom of the screen.

Richard walks to the desk and pickhe scorpion. “Meet Serqet. She’s what you paid for.“

Wilde moves forward and crouches down to look at the bug.

“A little power in a lot of hands will make the world a wonderful place. That's what the colors on the computer say. This little bug never needs batteries. It collects and stores just enough power for its needs.”

Wilde reaches to take the bug and gets a sharp shock. He clutches his burned hand with wide-eyed surprise.

Richard rolls his hand from side to side and the scorpion smoothly follows the movement.

“It’s a toy,” says Wilde.

“You were thinking big, Dr. Wilde. Eddie was thinking small. You wanted power you could control. Eddie wanted power everywhere. Harvesters work too well. Once tuned to the resonant frequency, power collection starts. If it's not used, and can't be stored or discharged fast enough, the system melts down. Something small like Serqet can run forever because it never overwhelms it's storage capacity. And even if it did, you'd have a minor accident not a disaster.”

“Fine,” says Wilde. “Where are the plans?”

“Right about now, I'd say they were everywhere,” says Richard.

Wilde looks at him, but Richard looks at Paige.

“It was a bomb. I was the trigger. All I had to do was let it go. Eddie gave me a bargaining chip but I couldn't bring myself to use it. I thought about trading my life, our lives, for his technology. But I don't want people like him to run the world anymore.”

Richard turns to look at Widle and says, “You know, the history of the world really is written by unreasonable people.”

There’s an explosion that rocks the building. The lights go off all at once and now only fire illuminates the lab. Richard walks away from the window and toward Paige.

“I'm sorry I couldn't do the right thing. You deserve better than a Maxwell. We all have a messiah complex.”

“What are you talking about? You did the right thing. How could you do anything less?” she replies.

“I didn't think you had it in you,” says Duane.

“Eddie was right about you. Your heart was always in the right place.”

Wilde, staring at his lab, points at the part of four. “Arrest them Colonel. We'll see how happy they are spending the rest of their lives in a federal prison.”

Colonel White, illuminated by electrical flashes, looks from Wilde to Richard to Wilde again. He turns to his men. “Let's head out, Boys. Base security can take it from here.”

Oscar, Paige and Duane race toward hangers at the far side of the airfield. Behind them smoke is billowing.

“Those Harvesters sure put on a great show,” says Oscar.

“That they do,” replies Richard.

“It would never have occured to me to blow them up in batches,” says Duane.

Left alone, Wilde is watching his machines melt

and deform. The roof above the lab has torn open. Pale stars illuminate the sky and a gentle snow has started to fall.

CHAPTER 7

Six months later Richard and Paige are seated on the study couch watching TV. Paige is very pregnant and her head is against her husband's arm.

On screen, Oscar is demonstrating a water filtration unit on a national morning show. A small vaguely insectoid machine is lazily swimming in a big tank of dirty water rapidly becoming cleaner. "It can process hundreds of gallons of water in a day, and can operate without servicing for fifteen years. It forms the waste it collects into inert bricks that drop to the bottom of whatever body it's in. 3.5 million people die from unclean water every year. This unit has been adopted by forty one countries so far."

The host picks up another device and holds it up for the camera to view. "And what does this one do?"

"That creates heat. You can drop it into soup, or use

it to heat an oven. You can use a slightly larger version to heat a house. It shuts off at the temperature you specify or when it senses combustion. There's no need to burn coal, or gas, or use nuclear energy to turn turbines. We can deliver clean power anywhere."

The host puts the unit down. She picks up an object that looks a little bit like Eddie's scorpion. More utilitarian but still insect like.

"And all these products use the new Maxwell passive generator. It's hard to believe something so small can make such a big difference in such a short period of time."

"At Maxwell Brothers Engineering we like to say that a little power in a lot of hands will make the world a wonderful place."

BOOKS BY THIS AUTHOR

Fortunate Monsters

Who knew having a baby could be so darn dangerous? Roslyn and Jacob Kent, members of Hollywood's jet set, had every luxury money could buy except the ability to conceive on their own. Seeking a little elite fertility treatment wasn't supposed to put them at the mercy of a psychopath. Do you have to love your slightly demented kid less because he is a monster genetically engineered by a mad man? Maybe that's just a reason to love him more...

Nine Of Diamonds

Written by Judd Nelson & Nancy Fulton. A young girl presents problems for a hardened military interrogator.

Judd Nelson was born and raised in Portland, Maine. He currently lives in Los Angeles, California with two rescued pit bulls, and works as a professional actor. Nancy Fulton is a Los Angeles writer/producer, a wife of one and mother of three.

More At Audioiron.com

www.ingramcontent.com/pod-product-compliance
Lightning Source LLC
LaVergne TN
LVHW012104160826
845678LV00014B/2931
9798652754334